OF THE

ATERCOSM

(AND OTHER DARK
SPIRITS)

A COLLECTION

C.F. PAGE

Advance praise for *Orphans of the Atercosm*

"Page's writing is much like Lovecraft's oceans: glassy smooth in places, terrifyingly brutal in others, ever dark and full of mystery. *Atercosm* seduces with its eerie wonders and horrifies with its glimpses beyond the veil, where fathomless revelations linger just beyond our comprehension. Those who read this collection will encounter Page's unique brand of literary madness."

—Felix Blackwell,
bestselling author of *Stolen Tongues*

"A tour de force of the weird and the uncanny, C.F. Page's *Orphans of the Atercosm* is a must read for fans of Ligotti, Lovecraft, and all things weird horror."

—Richard Beauchamp,
author of *Black Tongue & Other Anomalies*

"I find that I have to prepare in advance to read a C.F. Page story because, once I begin, I know my responsibilities are going to fly out the window."

—Alana K. Drex,
author of *Sleeping Celeste* and *Shsskish*

"C.F. Page is a unique and gifted storyteller, and he's accomplished what very few authors have for me: aside from the fascinating story and interesting characters, Page manages to pull me back in through a unique and incredible writing style that I simply could not get enough of."

—Tobin Elliott,
author of the six-book horror series, *The Aphotic*

"*Orphans of the Atercosm* is a powerful reminder of why we must write horror. Page has a skillful mastery of structure and language, tormenting the reader the same way he torments his characters. This is a dark, cyclical exploration of the recesses of Page's mind, and the descent into his depravity is well worth it."

—**Aaron Beardsell,**
author of *Dead Station* and *Coffinwood*

Praise for *Native Fear*

"It's a beautiful, brutal, complex, terrifying read" (five stars).

—*Scream Magazine*

"Page's *Native Fear* is a blistering and evocative examination of man's darkness. A harrowing read."

—**Steve Stred**,
Splatterpunk-nominated author of *Sacrament* and
Mastodon

"Debut author [C. F.] Page presents an intricate horror novel . . . an inventive take on a rural place filled with unspeakable malice."

—*Kirkus Reviews*

"Page knows exactly how to write a psychedelic horror tale . . . John Carpenter's *The Thing* meets Nick Cutter's *The Troop* meets *Cabin in the Woods.*"

—**Thomas Gloom**
author of *The Potted Plant, Voodoo Child,* and *The Window*

(SIDE A)

THE
LIGHTHOUSE

CONTENTS

APOCALYPSIS

"Did I request thee, Maker, from my clay to mold me man? Did I solicit thee from darkness to promote me?"

—JOHN MILTON, *PARADISE LOST*

ORPHANS OF THE ATERCOSM

U HOB-AW UHOT)

And then there was an EBON tinge over Us all when a voice, paternal and endless, said no more. Before the end, the last rays of day—of narrative—hovered above OUR axiomatic sacrament of redblack wastelands and near-sunless seas of febrile salt lined with rotten LIGHTLESS lighthouses. It absconded *ad astra* from the earth that's bursting from its seams, full of excess, with its decrees and edicts; an *aborted* work.

And then the hungry DARK, in the day's absence, swallows the last curlicue of sunlight and spews out from its mouth a hue of foul NIGHT.

And then the remaining misaligned and tormented ORPHANS, which were forged in the fires of OUR own ABYSS, creep out from grottos *ad nauseam*—dolmens of bone and dust, of steel and concrete—monolithic rubble of oblique, quiet horrors—graveyards of diseased, sun-baked *Loxodonta* and diseased, gang-raped *Equus asinus asinus*, and decaying vestiges of brutish mothers and frail fathers, thieves and murderers, liars and shamans, exorcists, and countless children covered in alabaster ash, scantily clothed if at all, whose bedtimes and meals and messes are forever evaded, wasted, and remain—

And then an imaginal miasma of decrepit city ruins splays out before OUR eyes of contorted imago effigies

(*screaming sobbing slobbering, a discordant litany*)

(*self-absorbent, -tormented, -worshiped*

[sweltering; boiling; all-consuming]

souls)

in OUR truest forms. That of vacant manikins, homes for invited grotesqueries. A slow-boiling cesspool frothing with corrupted VOID, indwelt by the spirit of Belial. WE're like blind, mad idiots searching for Leviathan's teat, with an inchoate instinct to exploit its milk—an *exegesis* of the supernal and the mortal coil.

And then an unfurling of corpulent pandemonium—a tourniquet to stave the cancerous supposition of WE, the ORPHANS OF THE ATERCOSM.

The sun flickers.

The stars, o the stars, blink, blink out.

Blink in, then out.

Fade fast. Retract.

Fade forever. Rescind.

Flicker and flicker, a disintegration of star dust and antimatter. And they reform, new, a star, a morning. An antilight genus—so bright—pulls about OUR world its NIGHTGLOW and a spirit of metanarcissism and loveless lust, of oversexed avarice and pain-tainted eroticism.

And then, to roost, the SERPENTS come.

—**WANDERING PROPHET OF THE LUNARIS DEVERSORIUM, *THE PASSAGE OF OSLO* [TRANSLATED TO ENGLISH]**

ORGANISM

"Ph'nglui mglw'nafh Cthulhu R'lyeh wgah'nagl fhtagn."

—H.P. LOVECRAFT

"And if you gaze long enough into an abyss, the abyss will gaze back into you."

—FRIEDRICH NIETZSCHE

THE GLOBSTER OF CAPE FRANKFURT

—*for H. P. Lovecraft & Stephen King*

I

I T'S REASONABLE THAT YOU HADN'T heard about the organism—or "globster" (all the cool kids use that term nowadays)—found at Cape Frankfurt in 1978. It never made headlines: and that, I believe, is by design.

I was fifteen. Apprenticed with Dr. Isherwood, the only veterinarian at Cape Frankfurt—which was even by today's standards a microscopic fishing village. Some people called him Dr. Tic Tac. It's because he gave out Tic Tacs to the kids. Always the orange flavored, never the gross mint kind. But because of my apprenticeship and my conservative upbringing (not to mention my intrinsic nature, perhaps), I called him "Sir" or "Boss" or "Doctor." Never Dr. Tic Tac.

It was the morning after a big storm in July when the phone rang. I remember this. A tree had smashed Dad's boathouse to smithereens. That's why I was five minutes late—I had to help Dad pick up the splinters and transfer them to the bed of his Chevy pickup—and I remember the sheer panic I felt when I entered the clinic (a mere renovated barn on his property), located about two miles outside city limits, when I observed the tightness of his mouth and the hard look in his eyes over the rim of his eyeglasses. I'm quite certain he was about to teach me a "hard lesson about tardiness," and I would have accepted the lesson without complaint—

Luckily that was when the phone rang.

Dr. Isherwood answered.

His face changed.

He said, "Have you been drinking? A *what*—? Okay, okay, fine. *Okay*, I said."

He looked over at me—a strange, vacant stare.

To the caller he said, "*We'll* be there as soon as we can."

II

WYOMING CONTAINS LESS THAN ONE per cent water. It's one of the driest states. As the crow flies, it's approximately nine hundred and sixteen miles from the nearest ocean. I live there now, in a small town near the state's center.

III

HE'D BROUGHT ME ALONG IN case they needed a strong arm. That's what he'd told me in the truck (also a Chevy—Dad's was white and newer; Dr. Isherwood's was black and rusted).

"With what?"

"I'm not sure."

"What did Mr. O'Neil say?"

Dr. Isherwood—a man who always kept his eyes forward when he drove, and with hands at ten and two, a man who didn't even listen to the radio for it was a distraction—*well*—and sometimes I still have nightmares about not necessarily the two words he uttered but the way he shifted his hands and contorted his customary quasi-military posture and the way he looked at me in his pickup (a couple weeks ago was the last time I conjured this memory in my dreamscape, so as I write this it feels like yesterday)—*well*, he said this:

"A monster."

IV

I KNOW WHAT YOU'RE THINKING.

If this is the first time you've heard of the term "globster," no doubt you've typed that eight-letter word into your Google search. *Unidentified organic mass that's washed up on a shoreline.* You're probably thinking, *Old Man, that's in the same ballpark as a UFO—unidentified means nothing sinister.*

You may furthermore have discovered via research that the St. Augustine Monster (1896) was identified as a whale carcass; that the Tasmanian Globster (1960) was identified as a whale carcass; and that the New Zealand Globster (1965), Bermuda Blob (1988), Nantucket Blob (1996), Bermuda Blob 2 (1997), and the Chilean Blob (2003) were all identified—conveniently so—as whale carcasses. Ergo—surmising in your head, no doubt—you assume also that the Cape Frankfurt Globster (1978) was too just a decomposing slab of whale carcass.

And you may also have noticed that the year 1978 was only three years after *Jaws*, which was the film that defined the term "Blockbuster," and that maybe, because of the film's lingering popularity, the folk of Cape Frankfurt's imaginations were just going *wild*; and that the suicides which would come in less than a week's time were just a form of the sociological phenomenon called "mass hysteria."

Dear reader, here's an exercise to flex your brain:

Do you *honestly* believe that the seasoned fisher- and boatmen who lived near those shorelines in the years 1896, 1960, 1965, 1988 (the year I was married by the way—she wanted to go to Hawaii on our honeymoon, but we went to Colorado; we're divorced now, no kids), 1996 and '97, and 2003 could not tell the difference between a whale and . . . well, *something else*?

Do you *honestly* believe the "official" identifications of these organisms from government-funded "experts" who are yoked to the ones who to this day *still* insist that most of our calories should come from grains?

Listen:

When Dr. Isherwood said, "A monster," I rolled my eyes. Like you—although the term "globster" was not yet in my brain's diction room—I too thought it must have been a carcass of a whale or a shark or a squid. What else could it have been?

I ALTERED THIS HYPOTHESIS WHEN I finally saw the sea matter.

V

OLD MAN HENRY LIVED ON the slab of land for which the town was named: the cape. The ridge stood above the ocean with its rocky sides nearly vertically rushing into the water. Waves sloshed against the rock, making the lower portions look almost black except for the blue-green moss and other upward-crawling marine organisms. And at the corner of this nearly water-surrounded stretch of land lay a wasted lighthouse. It hadn't been in operation for decades and the path which led to it was hidden by greedy, weedy vegetative stuff.

Although my memory is fuzzy now, I imagine that when I opened Dr. Isherwood's passenger side window the sound from the rock-sloshing waves had been the equivalent to sticking a mighty conch—maybe even Poseidon's conch, if he had one—up to my ear.

Constant. Hypnotic. Uncanny.

Fortunately (or unfortunately—it's hard to say for certain), three of O'Neil's grandsons—all of them five or six years older than I, and each with jockish muscularity which trumped my one hundred and sixty pounds soaking wet—stood next to the shriveled form of their grandfather on the shore to our left. Even from where I'd been sitting I made out the curious shape half-floating in the water, the other half haphazardly crumpled onto land like a soggy carpet. Its fine details were obscured by at least a hundred meters; even so, it was plain as differentiating night from day that what spilled onto land—from what my dreams have ever since depicted as a dark, deep, disheartening abyss—was unlike anything I'd ever seen.

"Stay in the truck," said Dr. Isherwood. (I wonder, now, if some part of him *knew* what would happen if I came too close.)

9

My love of animals (especially marine life) coupled with my current intrigue, albeit of a frightful variety, caused me to protest. He gave me a hard glare and I immediately protested no more.

I kept the window open so I wouldn't die of heatstroke—remember, it was July.

The wind carried their voices. I heard one of the pillars of muscle say "Dr. Tic Tac" (although not very loudly), and then the smack across the back of his head from his grandfather's open hand. "Sorry. *Dr. Isherwood*," he corrected himself. I'm pretty sure that was Ivan Ullman, Old Man Henry's married daughter's son. I heard that he killed himself a couple years later; he was the only of the grandsons who hadn't been taken by sea that very week. (As for the reason why Ivan wore gloves but John and Bill O'Neil didn't, I can only speculate that he was either what we call a "germophobe"—or he was more sensible. I theorize it had extended his life for those few years. But I wonder if it was quality life.)

During their struggle pulling out and lifting the agglomerative organism, I kept hearing what I can only describe as nails on a chalkboard. No, it didn't *actually* sound like that; it's only a sort of . . . placeholder-simile. Has more to do with the irksome effect it had on me. Even to this day I can't quite describe it, except to say it was a . . . *flupping* sound.

Feeling uneasy, I rolled up the window and decided enduring the super sauna was better than the

(*flup*

flup

flup)

alternative. Better than that godforsaken noise. Although while I didn't quite *hear* it in the sealed inferno, I *felt* it. Felt the vibration of the ~~fucking~~ *flupping* sound permeating through the window like eldritch

10

radiation.

For a little while, after they had successfully lifted the shape into the truck, Dr. Isherwood and Old Man Henry spoke. Window up, I couldn't hear; but when the doctor made his way back, I rolled the window back down. I didn't want him asking why I'd willingly made an oven for myself, because I wouldn't have had a rational answer.

As Old Man Henry and his grandsons piled into the Ford and made a backward U-turn, Dr. Isherwood opened the door, plopped on the seat, sat there quietly.

"What was it?"

I noticed how white Dr. Isherwood's face was.

His mouth opened hesitantly. I think subconsciously he was about to say the m-word again but altered that course of thinking at the last second. Instead he said the most intellectual, sensible response. "I haven't the slightest idea."

VI

MARY WANTS ME TO WRITE all this down—the Event which led to the psychological condition I have, the one which Google calls "aquaphobia." Mary's my therapist. She thinks that writing it down might make it easier for me to discuss the Event during one of our sessions. Of course she knows nothing of the globster, or how Dr. Isherwood held hands with Old Man Henry, and how Old Man Henry held hands with Fake Richard Dreyfuss (I'll get to *him* in a moment), how he held onto Dad's hand, and so forth and so on, and how they, all twelve of them, walked into the cold, dark nothingness; nor does she know how I lost my left hand's pinky, ring, and index

11

finger.

But she knows that what happened is why I'm so damned thirsty.

She also tells me to keep a dream journal.

I've attempted this. But I . . . how would I say it? I lie. I embellish. If I dream about the cold black, I write about the undead. If I dream about the cold black, I write about skyscrapers. If I dream about the cold black, or a bioluminescent fin of some unknowable leviathan therein, or a small red speck which might be the sun, or the dim smudge of a pickled jack-o-lantern grin (of not an anglerfish but what anglerfish have nightmares of)—then I write about puppies or forgetting my locker combination and homework or going to school in my birthday suit.

Basic, common dreams.

VII

DAD BUILT HOUSES AMONG OTHER things.

So it only made sense when Dr. Isherwood called him and requested a most simple project (this one I actually did assist my dad with, despite Ivan Ullman and John and Bill O'Neil being present; he told me later they didn't actually *need* my help but thought I could use calluses on my hands; he said, "You've got soft writer's fingers, but you're not a writer"), which was to build a shed.

But first I guess it's necessary for you to understand *why*: they wanted to preserve the globster, of course. They thought it could have been the find of the century.

Old Man Henry and his three behemoth grandsons took Dr. Isherwood's pickup truck and went to the supermarket and bought a kiddie pool and two dozen big bags of ice. The shed had to be big enough to fit the pool, with enough additional space to assemble the pool inside it.

While Dad and I and the meatheads built the shed, Dr. Isherwood and Old Man Henry filled the Ford's bed with ice to preserve the organism. The sky was overcast, it had cooled down considerably since morning, so there was minimal melting of the ice—and the tarp assisted furthermore.

After the shanty was assembled, which took five hours, Dad and Dr. Isherwood and Old Man Henry went inside with lanterns and assembled the pool. We stayed outside. The O'Neils never said a word to me. They were too preoccupied looking underneath the tarp and giggling like schoolgirls (I think Bill held onto Samantha Riley's hand, and John held Father James's hand). Eventually Ullman asked if he could use Dr. Isherwood's restroom and I said yes.

We waited.

It didn't take long till the adults finished assembling the pool. I waited at a distance while Ullman (wearing his gloves once again, which, like I said, undoubtedly added a couple years to his life), the O'Neils, Dr. Isherwood, and Dad carried the organism from the bed of the Ford to the pool inside the shed. Afterward, they filled buckets with ice from the Ford and filled the pool.

That's the first time I saw the globster in high definition: it looked like a colony of bees had made a nest across the surface of carpet which furthermore had been corroding and rotting and moldering in some dark, dank, unthinkable place for half an eternity. In other words: nothing special. But that sound it made, my God. That *flup* . . .

. . . *flup* . . .

13

. . . *flup.*

My crotch felt warm. Then wet. Then it was my turn to use Dr. Isherwood's bathroom. I stripped down. Took my urine-soaked underwear and shoved it at the bottom of the trashcan, so when Isherwood changed it he'd be none the wiser.

VIII

THE OTHER DAY MARY HAD asked me—in a walking-on-eggshells sort of way—if it would be *maybe* okay for her to drink water in front of me.

Obviously I said, "No."

She knew I'd say no, of course, but I also knew this was a test. Then, measuredly passive: "I'm sorry for stepping over your boundaries—but I am thirsty. Is there a beverage you would allow me to consume—that wouldn't upset you?"

After a cerebral typhoon of calculations, inferences, and philosophical conjectures, I said—however ridiculous (but I did have my reasons; I never say or do anything without reasons—if you've been reading carefully, you would know this about me)—"Apple cider would be acceptable."

Not apple juice. Water was added to it, among other things; on the other hand, cider was pure, unadulterated apple blood.

She made a sound. Not quite a sigh.

"I'm sorry. We don't have apple cider at the office."

She paused.

I knew what beverages they had at the office; and I had a pretty good idea what she was going to ask permission for her to drink—or rather, I deduced the improbabilities of what wouldn't be in the office (e.g., milk, alcohol, battery acid) and what would be in the office but she'd know better than to ask (e.g., juices, cold brews, water).

"What about coffee?" Her eyebrow raised. She wanted to see my reaction before presenting her argument. But I had already assessed the improbabilities of contamination (I guess my reasoning, however illogical—which wasn't to say, by some degree, the phobia as a whole wasn't illogical—was that if ITS particles happened to have been mixed into the water via whatever unlikely—but you certainly can't say "impossible"—chain-of-butterfly-effect-events, then the heat *might* have killed IT, or IT may have bound ITSELF to the coffee grounds in the filter and not have entered the drinkable coffee-essenced water in the pot, etc., etc., etc. . . .), and besides, I didn't want to hear her pitiful begging.

So I said, "Fine."

What happened next was involuntary. It was not an act. In fact, after she had done so, she quickly put her hands down and stilled them between her slender thighs.

She had clapped. Her eyes told me she thought we were making progress. Really *really* good progress.

I knew there was a slight chance she was contaminated already, that IT may have parasitically inserted ITSELF into her brain, and one day IT may use her body as a vessel to abduct me and bring me back to Mother. What she didn't know was that this was my last session; but it *was* good progress, I'll grant her that. Like how therapy might make a married couple come to terms with the necessity of divorce, this session—my *allowing* her to drink coffee and my *accepting* the risk—helped my decision to go to the hardware store and buy rope.

She thought *she* was thirsty. That's adorable.

I haven't had a beverage since I accidently swallowed some salt water while trying to pull Dad away.

That's when I lost my fingers.

IX

ONLY TWO OTHER TIMES IN my two-year apprenticeship had I found Dr. Isherwood anywhere other than his barn-clinic. The first time, he'd overslept; the second time, he'd gotten a stomach bug and was glued to the toilet in his house, in which he'd told me to go home and take the rest of the day off; then reporting to work the day after the globster's discovery was the third time. On that Sunday, after I'd gone to church—the only time Dr. Isherwood had allowed me to show up later than nine *ante meridiem*—I found Dr. Isherwood in the shed. I knew he'd been there even before knocking on the door (which, I have to say—even after all these years later, I remember my awe at Dad's craftsmanship—was a sturdy door with a higher quality of wood than any temporary, makeshift shed had the right of having), because I had heard a noise: a strong, unnatural wind— *Euroclydon*—pulled his whisperings from underneath the door. And while the north wind seemed to carry his voice to my ears, it also distorted the words. Turned it to a mushy red noise.

I knocked.

Waited.

Knocked again.

Heavy, frantic footfalls—an instinct told me to back away. I did. The door swung open. For a moment I knew not the man who stood before me—unshaven, raccoon eyes, untucked shirt, and what appeared to be water or sweat stains across his chest, abdomen, and thighs.

He said my name thrice—unbelievingly, blinkingly—and then, like Noah's reaction when his son saw him drunk and naked (which was what Pastor James had taught about not even two hours earlier)—embarrassment and anger flooded his face.

"What are you doing?" he said to me, slamming the door shut.

"It's"—I looked at my cheap wristwatch—"time to work."

"No work, not today." He paused. "Maybe not tomorrow or the next day."

Turning around swiftly, he reached for the door-knob; and during this ridiculous movement I opened my mouth to ask him if he was okay (the subtext being *in his head*, of course), but a horn blared out. He took his hand away from the knob, looked at his wrist, whispered something—

"*Ahoy there*," came a familiar voice from a familiar car.

Hurriedly Dr. Isherwood shambled across his (as of just recently) unkempt yard and greeted the speaker and gestured him out of the car. It was Pastor James, who, upon seeing me, said my name, and, while passing by, ruffled my hair. Pastor James said to Dr. Isherwood, "You said you wanted to . . . *show me something*, doctor?"

Dr. Isherwood nodded frantically and ambled back across his yard to the shed with nary a glance over his shoulder, and Pastor James followed at a slower, less frantic pace. He opened the shed door and curtly nodded toward the shadow-infested open doorway.

"Come in."

Pastor James entered the shed, and a few days later he, too, would succumb to the Madness.

PASTOR RICK FILLED IN FOR Pastor James the following week; that Sunday would be the last church sermon I'd ever go to. It still fascinates me to this day how quickly the hospital will try to release you after losing a few fingers. At any rate, it had been a communion day. They handed out juice and crackers. I remember holding that juice with the hand which was liberally dressed in bandages; remember looking into that small cup whose surface was flat and rubescent and so very deep that it must've went well beyond the cup's bottom; remember seeing IT with ITS congregation floating in that red, in that gore, sinking down and down and down into the unknowable depths of the abyss.

X

MY DEFINITIONS DISSOLVE IN SOME kind of cosmic obscurity—a suffocating coffinlike encasement—and I can't seem to find myself in that stuff, whatever it is: the quintessence of cold, wet darkness—it's water, and it's not water. I reach out gropingly, sweeping my arms back and forth. My hand brushes against something. Someone's pruned appendage. Maybe a rotted face. You'd think I'd be able to reach backward, toward where the joints of my arms are connected to—which is to say my shoulders—but we're now, both you and I, in a place where that kind of logic is senseless, where there is no north or south, no gravity, and up is as up as it is down, which is to say neither. I've already tried reaching inward. My hands feel nothing except for ITS abysmal anatomy.

Then I woke up in bed. That's where I'd been. Many leagues away from that terror. And many decades later.

Only three fingers were freezing: the ones I don't have anymore.

I pulled out my dream journal. This time I considered writing the truth, the whole truth, and nothing but . . .

. . . then it occurred to me why, in the Bible, Jesus always spoke in metaphors—because, as Nicholson once said, "You"—all of mankind—"can't handle the truth." Same reason why when angels appeared they always said, "Be not afraid," because sometimes the truth, and the shape it takes, can be petrifying.

SOMETHING RUSTLED OUTSIDE MY BEDROOM window.

It *flupped.*

I should think it wise to keep the lights on until dawn.

XI

BY THE END OF THE third day Cape Frankfurt buzzed with gossip. That Dr. Isherwood had invited someone's friend's dad to see a previously undiscovered sea creature. That someone's cousin's boyfriend was summoned, too, said it was clearly a thing not of this earth. That Coach Mills of the Varsity football team said it was almost Biblical ("how so?" I heard someone ask at the grocery store;

"he said it sang a song in his brain, sounded like a hymn";

"that's impossible," I heard that first someone say;

19

but I didn't think it was impossible, and as a church-goer—although by no means a scholar, but I did pride myself in having an unusually matured level of discernment for my age—I knew there was *nothing* strictly speaking Biblical about the globster). But as I sit here waiting for dawn, I admit there certainly were some correspondences to a religious awakening. For instance, the abnormally too-well-crafted shed and the painstaking efforts that Dad, Dr. Isherwood, and Old Man Henry put into it, now remind me of Leviticus; the Hebrews, in order to effectively communicate with God—to quasi-literally "*contain*" God—had to construct a tabernacle with anally particular measurements and materials. Or else.

(*Death.*)

Then, after its construction was complete, people had to make super precise, super specific sacrifices for blessings and forgiveness. Or else.

(*Death.*)

Was Dr. Isherwood like Moses? Had he received systematized instructions *from* the globster—first in the construction of the shed, then in . . .

. . . bringing witnesses?

(*And Death. And things much much* much *worse than Death.*)

Rumors fermented into confused conspiratorial thinking, but the truth was stranger and darker than what sane minds could fathom and fabricate.

On the fourth day of the globster, I reported to work. While Dr. Isherwood *studied* the globster (at least that's what I had told Mrs Carlisle who wanted her barn cats dewormed; I had to do it by myself, reassuring her that Dr. Isherwood let me do this, self-supervised, many times—obviously a lie), I heard a knock on the clinic's door.

My neck hairs stood on end. Everyone in Cape Frankfurt simply knew to just enter. No one knocked until that day.

I crossed the clinic on legs that felt like stilts, my arm stretched forward, and my hand found the knob and twisted and revealed two men. The strong wind walloping against the clinic's aluminium sides had roused a colony of obstreperous gulls. The shoreline was two miles away, but these gulls hung out at the parking lot of an Amish-owned grocery store kitty-corner from Dr. Isherwood's residence. The juxtaposition between the interior of the dimly lit clinic and the bright afternoon which stood the two men, both wearing forest-green fisherman beanies (like the one Richard Dreyfuss wore in *Jaws*), not to mention the gulls swirling about the salty air above and between the palm trees over their shoulders at some distance away, with their purring grunting squawking laughing crooning crying squealing hooting cooing, made me half-imagine the beach was just around the corner.

The younger of the two introduced himself and the other, older man—obviously fake names—and said they were marine biologists (when the older of the two shifted his body to shake my hand, I saw a gun on his hip holster), and that they had heard, "through the grape-vine" (he chuckled), that there had been a discovery of "a very *strange animal*. And supposedly your boss—his name's Dr. Isherwood, correct?—well, I guess he's the man to see." That was the only part I believed; with the sheer volume and viralness of our town's gossip, I wouldn't have been surprised if President Carter had caught wind.

I can't remember the younger one's fake name, but let's call him Fake Richard Dreyfuss—and I think, be-cause of *Jaws'* success three years earlier, they—

21

whoever *they* were (government, private sector, men in black)—probably had a focus group in which they concluded that if they brought in a man who resembled Richard Dreyfuss from *Jaws*, and dressed like him too, that the dumb Cape Frankfurt civilians would like and trust him instantly.

I didn't like him; he smiled too much.

I liked the older one, the one who didn't smile, the one whose face had a redness to it, like he was waiting for a reason to be mean: I'll call him the Irascible Man.

"Can we, um, speak to your boss?" asked Fake Richard Dreyfuss while rubbing his hands giddily.

My gut instinct told me that if I didn't invite them in, that maybe the charades would promptly dissolve and the Irascible Man would find a reason to pull out the gun on me; so I invited them in, asked if they'd like coffee. "Not after midday," said Fake Richard Dreyfuss. I could tell that the Irascible Man *did* want some but also didn't want a reason to "like me" just in case he needed to pull out the pistol and make a small dark circle in the center of my forehead.

"At the moment, he's *studying* the, um, animal," I told them.

"In here?"

"Not in here. There's a shed in the backyard."

"It's in a *shed*?"

"A *big* shed," I told Fake Richard Dreyfuss. "There's a pool in the shed. Keeps ice in it, too."

"Is it alive?"

I opened my mouth to respond, except I had realized that I didn't know the answer to that question. Part of me wondered how something that looked like that could be alive; at the same time, how could something dead make that *flup flup flup* sound?

"Have you touched it?" the Irascible Man asked me,

22

his voice a tin can full of shook marbles, his hand instinctively going to his hip, his face redder, meaner.

"I've only seen it at a distance," I said.

My face must have betrayed me because Fake Richard Dreyfuss said:

"Did it frighten you?"

What a strange thing to ask about a thing which any sensible person would not be afraid of. A shark—even a jellyfish—was literally scarier than the globster, although literalness and objectivity were in the outer rim of my psyche regarding the "very strange animal."

"It creeps me out—especially how Dr. Isherwood reacts to it," I said. Actually I was hoping they'd take away the doctor's obsession, that way my life would return to normal.

"How so?"

"Strange. Irritable. Hasn't shaved in four days, which is rare because he's a vet—the *other* kind of vet, I mean. A military vet. And he's been showing the animal to people. In secret."

The two men looked at one another.

I showed them to the shed. I knocked. Had to yell out Dr. Isherwood's name several times before he opened the door. He was more disheveled than ever. A mangy nautical prophet. And an inhuman stench— vegetal and of old, *forgotten* decay—had imbedded itself into his clothes and skin and hair.

XII

IF MARY READS MY NEW entry, she'll think I had a nightmare about being buried alive with a dozen other people. This coffin is large and spongy like honeycombs, and

23

there are thin, stringy tendrils inserting themselves into all our bodies, connecting our nervous systems to Mother Coffin. It's thousands of feet below the surface and vertical and deceptively long-reaching like a light-house, its lantern the shape of an oil-black

(*eye*)

orb. Only worms and unnameable eyeless things slither down here. All the corpses in this dream are vaguely sentient of their pitiful half-existence.

This entry is the closest I've ever been to telling Mary the dark truth.

Listen:

I know you look down on me. You think I'm crazy. I'm just the neighbor or the distant relative that had gone batshit crazy and removed all his sinks and faucets; who uses baby wipes to shower; who refuses to drink water and most beverages (almost all food has traces of water, so don't you go thinking I'm a cactus); who won't step out of his house when it rains and will wait until the ground dries up before walking on it; or who might, when trudging down a sidewalk (I'm not a complete recluse; I *do* go to psychotherapy once a week), scream at a puddle of water or flat-out, uncontrollably piss himself. I'm just the guy who's petrified of water is how you look at me.

Shame on you for being so ignorant.

The Abyss never leaves me; and I never leave it. It has three of my fingers, and if you were to scratch off the healed portion of my nubs, you'd see a spongy material. And when my body is taken to the coroner, I'm certain they'll discover a trail of that substance has stretched out from my nubs all the way to my brain.

That spongy bodily invader makes the

    (. . . *flup* . . .
        . . . *flup* . . .

24

. . . flup . . .)

same sound. A few hours ago I tossed the rope over the rafters of my log cabin-style house. That was one of my requirements to the real estate agent I'd hired when I moved here. For this very specific reason. I knew one day IT would find me, but I wouldn't give IT the satisfaction of ending me on ITS terms: or, rather, never letting me end, as my father and Dr. Isherwood and Henry, John, and Bill O'Neil, and Pastor James and Fake Richard Dreyfuss are still out there, unendingly part of ITS aquatic assembly.

I was there when what the news called "a spell of mass hysteria" happened, which, according to them, had nothing—"absolutely nothing, folks," Sheriff Olney had said to the journalists, "so let's respect our departed loved ones by not partaking in this conspiratorial thinking"—to do with the "rotted whale carcass" discovered. (Of course it was a whale—it's always a whale.)

You can hear it, can't you?

XIII

I WOULD LIKE TO TELL you that several days after the globster's initial discovery IT had somehow escaped the pool in Dr. Isherwood's shed; that IT tumbled from household to household like a demented man-eating blob and collected disciples to ITS posse; that on the sixth day I was holed up in Mr. Peterson's gun store, that we had to fend off against the mind-controlled Romeroian zombies, and one of them bit off my fingers; that there was a dip in the climatic showdown when Fake Richard Dreyfuss, fatally injured, warned me that an evil company, or a shady government group, was on their way and would kill the entire populace to procure the escaped bioweapon or alien or whatever; and that during this cinematic apex I saved the hottest girl in my school (which had been Patricia Heatherson: I heard she got lung cancer a few years back and passed away) and that we fell in love and she wanted to go with me inland, but I told her, "Sweetheart, you've got a life to live—and, anyway, I've got to do this on my own."

But none of that happened; and contrary to the law of Chekhov's gun, I don't even think the Irascible Man used his gun on anyone or anything, perniciously or otherwise; and I think that's what I hate so much about what happened.

The sheer mundanity of the whole affair.

It happened like this:

One morning, before dawn, I heard a noise.

It was Dad.

I said something to him—some kind of joke, I can't remember what, only that he didn't respond. He had nothing on except for his boxer briefs and a wifebeater. I also remember asking where he was going, but again he said nothing and he left the house without his keys or wallet, let alone a jacket or slip-ons, and I quickly got dressed and followed. We lived a quarter mile from the shore, so it didn't take long. I also spied another figure walking, but it was too dark and foggy to see his or her identity.

I tried to snap my dad out of it. Tried grabbing onto his arm. He said my name once, I think. Quietly. But didn't stop. Kept walking.

Another figure—Pastor James—came into view. He had the same braindead look my father had.

A group of twelve people (ten of them being Cape Frankfurt residents, the other two being the Irascible

26

Man and Fake Richard Dreyfus) met on the beach. Now the pink-orange sun rose. I could see as they circled around something that the *something* was the globster; and they each, meticulously separating themselves equal distances, grabbed a corner of the organism. As soon as their fingers touched its terrible membrane, it *flupped* and *flupped* like a demented metronome, like a dog wagging its tail excitedly, like Hell Bongos, as if human touch was what activated the sound. They lifted it easily, almost romantically.

The twelve hummed nonsensical hymns as they walked into the water. I followed at a safe distance, calling out for my father, for Dr. Isherwood (I even tried "Dr. Tic Tac" but to no avail), for Pastor James, for anyone to snap out of it. I hadn't realized there was a group of about thirty others who had followed me, who were witnessing this strange mass suicide which would soon be called THE MADNESS by the local news. Some of them were, no doubt, loved ones who also didn't understand why Mom or Dad were randomly leaving the house just before sunrise.

I swam after them. Reached for Dad but my hand slipped and fell into a thousand grinding razor blades. At first I saw only red. Then, from the spongy surface of the globster, an oil-black eye—and at its center a pupil the color for which I have no name; it *felt* like red; it seared into my past, present, future. I'd seen that eye since before I was born; when I was five I'd dreamt about that eye and the color of its pupil; because, I suppose, I was always meant to see the eye. Had always seen the eye. Always will see the eye.

The pupil opened like a mouth.

Swallowed my three fingers, drank my blood; it wanted more, wanted *me*, but some part of Dad was still in there. He pulled me away from the *flupping* miscreation and said, "Now you've got calluses—"

—and before he could say one last thing (I could see it in his eyes and the way he opened his mouth), they had already submerged into the Abyss.

XIV

WHOEVER READS THIS, know that I hanged there, where there's a frayed rope looped from my living room rafter, for two weeks until the rope snapped. My hands are black with rot; I'm barely able to write this (forgive the finger on the desk; it had *dislodged* via whatever form of ecdysis which is transpiring; and I keep it there only for extraordinary evidence against my extraordinary claim), but I don't think I'm the one doing it. Writing, I mean. Where my three missing fingers—now four—had been nubs, there are now spongy things protruding. It wouldn't let me die after all.

Whoever reads this, you won't find me.

I'm going home so I can be with Mother Coffin.

PSYCHOSPHERE

"All are lunatics, but he who can analyze his delusion is called a philosopher."

—AMBROSE BIERCE

THE BOONDOGGLE

I. Dream Journals & Transcripts

BLUE JAYS

*T*HESE BIRDS ARE BLUE. *They dash from tree to tree in Grandma's backyard. They always seem to* yell *like they lost something or are looking for their hatchlings—or maybe just their eggs; hopefully they're still alive in their shells and not decaying in a pool of primordial, almostbird ooze—because they forgot where they'd nested them. Grandma on the balcony says they're songbirds, but whenever I crane my neck upward to ask* why *they'd sing* that *kind of song, I can only see the rails above the balcony looking over the land like a dark judgment, but not my Grandma, never my Grandma, not even a hand caressing the rail. Then she says: "They're called—scientifically, at least—Cyanocitta cristata, from the order of* Passeriformes, *from the family* Corvidae, *and they like acorns."*

—you nearly gave me a heart attack, Dr. Oakford. I didn't hear you come in.

These? You left them out on the table—

Yes, I understand your patients' info is confidential, but I obviously didn't know what I was reading until you just now told me. I thought maybe you started writing— well, I guess I don't know—a story, memoir, confession, whatever. Anyway, it's *your* fault for leaving them out, isn't it?

The entire thing is strange, Doc; I can't pick out just one thing. But if you insist, I guess the line about "primordial, almostbird ooze" is strangest. You could even say "off-putting." Everything else is par for the course when it comes to crazy people. Sorry, I suppose *mentally ill* is less derogatory . . . yet equally ominous, wouldn't you agree?

No, Doc. Like you said: this is confidential. And I've got stuff going on—

Since you're inquiring so obstinately, I was going to read for a few hours before bed. Don't smirk, Dr. Oakford; it's my ritual.

Well, I was curious was all. I thought *you'd* written it. It *does* look like your handwriting—see how the i's are dotted and the t's crossed? It's not that you shield your notetaking during our sessions. I'm sorry I snooped but I really don't have time to do your job for you.

Fine.

I said *fine,* didn't I? Shall I continue?

MOURNING DOVES

Apparently these birds like the morning but they're not Morning Doves. Grandma says they're a different kind of morning bird—with an extra "u." & they're sad. "That's why they make that sound, listen Child, hear that cooo-oo-oooo." Yes Grandma, I say, & she says something like, "Zenaida macaroni, Columbus forms Columbus

day," & when I crane my neck up to ask what any
of that means, I can see that above the rails of the
balcony, which looks over the backyard & all its
feathered inhabitants like a strange observer, are
layers upon layers of white cotton candy. Black
shapes of hands are stuck in that fluff.

Well, the handwriting looks different. For starters, if this had been the first page instead of the second page, I wouldn't have mistaken it for your handwriting. The i's are dotted differently (almost germ-shaped, squiggly and messy; distant dying stars come to mind), the t's are crossed with obnoxiously long lines, and the *ands* aren't written out. Not to mention that business about *Zenaida macaroni*. Seems like whoever wrote it misheard Grandma. Can you Google it? Mourning Doves. Yes. There. See: *Zenaida macroura*. The order is *Columbiformes*. The family is *Columbidae*.

I'd say that he has to be the same writer *despite* the handwriting appearing different. Don't laugh at me. *You're* the one asking for *my* help. I'm just saying, because the writer is talking about birds and his grandmother, it would make perfect sense for the writer to be the same person. Maybe he's writing differently on purpose.

What do I find disturbing? The cotton candy. The shapes of hands. The writer is misunderstanding what he's seeing.

Okay, if I read this one, please tell me what these pages are. Look at this, Doc! Whoever wrote this must be another doctor because I can hardly read it. Take my time! Doc, I don't have time; I've got very important work to do. If you understand what any of this scrawl means, then you read it. Here. Go ahead. I'll listen.

CARDINALS

They eat meat. Their feathers are drenched in blood because they burrow deep into carcasses so they can get the organs' vital nutrients. "Liver has as much vitamin C as most fruit," Grandma had once said, but not on this day; today she has the radio on and she's somewhere inside the house. Or maybe she's on the balcony watching but not responding. Or maybe she's not inside, not outside, but somewhere in-between, in the DREAM OF THE GREAT LIMINALITY. *I wonder if it's her hands I see in the cotton candy across the balcony rails.*

"Boondoggle doggle boondoggle doggle doggle doggle, doggle doggle," *the radio on the balcony sings out like a war cry to the Cardinals that look at me from their tree branch perches, their eyes black and beady and bleak, and they shoot invisible lasers from their black beaks as I stand there below Grandma's balcony, below the cotton candy that is now, I notice, seeping through the spaces between the baseboards. I see dark fingers wriggling through.*

"Boondoggledoggle," *sings the radio,* "boondoggledoggle."

You're pulling my leg, Doc. I won't say *that* word—I can't read any more of this nonsense about absolutely nothing. You know why, and it's disturbing besides. *Utterly* disturbing. Nobody thinks that Cardinals are red because they do *that.* Preposterous, *absolutely* preposterous. Sure, you work with the criminally insane, I get that, but, *wait*—you still haven't told me what these papers are, and I'm not going to read or listen to one more word until you tell me what's going on.

Are you saying the . . . the *B-word* . . . that it has killed *other* Grandmas? That I'm in here for no reason? (*Well* . . . you know what I mean.) These writings feel more like a prank than excerpts from dream journals. Shut up, Dr. Oakford! Stop reading. Don't say it. DON'T SAY THAT WORD!

CROWS

Many crows, and many more than many, sit like ebon voyagers on the rail of the balcony, which overlooks the land like a voyager.

"Boondoggledoggle, boon boon boon doggle doggle doggle."

Stop singing it like that, Doc. You can just read it normally for God's sake. It's upsetting me. *Why?* Because the only time I've ever talked about the *B-word* has been during *our* sessions.

What do they all have in common? You mean other than pure nonsense about absolutely nothing? I suppose there are recurring themes. Birds, grandma, and that godawful song. Oh. And the *balcony*. It's always described as looking out over the backyard, the birds, and the barn. It's nightmare fuel, Doc; there's just something *off* about it; no, I don't want to elaborate—

Why are you looking at me like *that*?

What about a barn? I didn't say anything about a barn.

No I didn't! I said that the balcony—in each of these dream journal excerpts—looks over the backyard and the goddamned fucking birds. That's all I said. I said nothing about a barn; and even if I did, I misspoke.

Just shut up and give that here, *John*. I'll keep reading if that means getting this over with and if that makes you happy.

RUBY-THROATED HUMMINGBIRDS

They buzz like bees.

   Buzzing blurs of green and red.
   They glitter like rubies in the morning sun.
   They drink nectar.

   *Grandma says, "They're called—scientifically, at least—*Archilochus colubris, *from the order* Caprimulgiformes, *from the family* Trochilidae.*"*

   Where are you, Grandma? *I ask.*

   *I see her hand—or what looks like a hand—except it has eight fingers—from over the rail—and a finger—a leg—points out and over and beyond and past the birds and into the crimson-flaking barn's open doorway, and this is what I see when I walk through the yard and peer inside the barn: nectar of strange effigies swelling up from the hay-littered ground . . . the setting sun bleeding through open slats of the weather-beaten, bat-infested rooftop . . . and motes dancing in and out of these phantasmagorical columns of dreamy light . . . and what the circles of not sun any longer but of moon show me (*THE GREAT LIMINALITY *from Day to Night had come like a thief) are winks of pale decay, wafts of sweet and spicy rot, and red and green blurs of wiggling mounds of—*
"Gang green," *says Grandma. Flies buzz around them.*

   (Also, "Voyager" is the wrong word to describe what those crows were doing; it's almost spelled like that but there's no "g," and there's a "u" somewhere in there—like the Mourning Dove.)

This one is written like a prose poem, mostly; there's an echo in it—like a figure eight made of words. They[1] also write in continuation of the previous dreamer, which means, Doc, that you're not telling me the truth. This *must* be the same writer or—maybe—yes—this could be a better explanation—a *different* writer that is aware of the previous writer's interpretation.

Isn't it obvious why I say that?

Voyager.

In the dream journal excerpt titled "Crows," the writer compares the murder to *voyagers*; however, the writer of "Hummingbirds" has an awareness of what had been written in the "Crows" dream, because they mention that the previous writer's usage of the word "Voyager" was wrong. They meant to say "Voyeur," and the "Hummingbirds" writer knew it.[2]

What's this one say?

[Laughter]

Is he[3] a little boy or something?

---

[1] Notice that this is the second major slip in the subject's narrative. The word "they" has a significant nexus to the dreamer's identity and our subject's slowly slipping mask of existential delusions.

[2] It's at this point that I considered pressing the subject on the use of the pronoun "they," but I decided to save this "card" for later. But considering what happened this morning, I regret withholding the question: I could have learned much about the subject's condition.

[3] "He" not "they."

OREOS

They look nothing like the cookie, except for their blacks and whites (the cookie doesn't have orange, obviously, and if it does you probably shouldn't eat it). And I'm hungry. And even from where I stand in the doorway of the barn where there are effigies in shallow graves buzzing with flies, I can't see Grandma on the balcony that looks over the backyard and the birds and the barn like a great and terrible eldritch skull, one which brims with a dreaming aura, its anatomy that of a smokeless chimney or a sealess light-house, time-eaten eaves, one mania-contaminated gable and the attic window below it, dormers and down spouts and cotton candy-caked windows and shutters, and brick, wood, and cement, and a balcony that looks over the backyard and the birds and the hunched figure in the barn loft, and me, like a great and terrible eldritch skull, one which brims with moony dreamlight, its anatomy that of—

I tell Grandma when I come back to the bottom of the balcony—where streams of cotton candy (and its eight-fingered hand-shaped passengers) whorl in rivulets down over the ledge, so long they'd touch the ground if not for their slowly undulating in the autumn wind—that I'm hungry, and Grandma tells me about—

This one has a cyclical nature, an ouroboros narrative, and a cul-de-sac of anything and everything which might help you feel at peace at night, dream *dreams* instead of nightmares, and wake up in the morning feeling well enough to put on your fancy suit and your fancy tie, Doc; it's pure and utter nonsense about absolutely nothing; and I'm getting quite ill reading these dreams. But if you insist, I'll read this one titled "Hirundo rustica"—*strange.*

Isn't it obvious?

Doc, don't be so dense.

I apologize. What I meant to say is: don't *pretend* to be dense.

Sure, I'll elaborate—for your tape recorder's sake. I'm a little out there, to be certain, Doc, but not unintelligent. I can almost guarantee that in your pocket is an audio recorder. And considering the ease in which you pulled out your phone to Google "sad birds" only means that you're an old-timey sort of fella, and you're using a *real* audio recorder instead of your phone.[4]

[*Sighs*]

In the previous six dreams—five, if you leave out "Oreos"—he used the common names of birds for their titles. In this next dream he used the scientific name.

HIRUNDO RUSTICA

Back in the barn.

I don't know who pointed toward the barn,

---

[4] It's at this point that the subject knows that I'm suspecting him of stalling and/or changing the trajectory of the conversation. He knows that I know that he knows, and yet we both turn a blind eye on the opaqueness of the buzzing silence. When the subject continues speaking, a dark quality infects his voice—there's a southern twang, and a bit of whistle between his teeth; it's as if the physiological structure of his mouth has altered in the span of that mutually analytical silence.

but it wasn't Grandma. Grandma hasn't been on the balcony—which looked over the backyard, its feathered inhabitants, and the barn (like an obscure confession)—for many more than a great many days. I can tell because of her face pressing up from the dirt from the ground in the barn. It almost *has something to do with the crows. Something about them damned black crows. So-god-damned-many of them, accusing me, harassing me with their interpretations.*

Nooselike weeds and other plants crawl up the sides of the barn as if the virid vegetation is starving and pulling that broken-down mausoleum down its gullet, snuffing it, hushing *it. The barn is sagging,* sinking, *being consumed by that which has awoken from whatever lay beneath. Its exterior is more gray than red, and the "gang green" stench is nothing but faint cinnamon.*

He's showing instead of telling us what *Hirundo rustica*'s common name is.

No, you can think *deeper* than that.

Very good. See, you didn't even need my help *digesting* that . . . consonance. Although I'm certain you've already Googled what *Hirundo rustica* means and you're only picking my brain—I'll forgive that.

Okay, Doc, okay.

[*Pages ruffle*]

The last dream. This'll take longer to read.

[*Clears throat*]

BOONDOGGLE

The Boondoggle is not A bird but, like birds, will tiptoe lightly on residential rooftops. The rooftops are usually "Grandma Rooftops," because most Grandmas watch birds, most Grandmas like birds, and most Grandmas talk about birds, and the Boondoggle, while not a bird (per se), watches, likes, and listens to Grandmas talk about birds. But unlike birds, it looks for unlatched windows (this Grandma had latched all her windows, alas causing the Boondoggle to find a more creative way of entry—that's why the Boondoggle uses a prybar [number one rule of the Boondoggle: always bring tools—e.g., prybar and hammer] to break into the attic just below the cotton candy- and handshape-festering gable, which furthermore is right above the balcony, the one that looks over the backyard, the birds, and the barn like an unconscious fantasist; the Boondoggle presses the prybar deeply and quietly into the gap between the attic windowpane and its frame and pushes this way, pulls that way, pushes, pulls, until it's loose and it does what it's supposed to do:

It pries open.

Then it enters the attic), and when the Boondoggle finds entry, conveniently or otherwise, it then assesses the "validity" of the Grandma. Searches with its many senses for evidence. Looks for doll collections, bowling paraphernalia, pool tables, grandfather clocks, wall clocks that make bird sounds ("ooo ooo, ooo ooo" or "tweet tweet, tweet tweet") at the top of the hour, or pictures of grandchildren; sniffs for cigarette smoke, mothballs, and "that old person smell that only manifests in households of octogenarians" because, and I quote, "it's the smell of the DREAM OF THE GREAT LIMINALITY*" (what that means, according to the Boondoggle, is none of your business*

. . . but you're welcome to guess); and listens for that mumbling sound of low-volume TVs. Usually it casts flickers of light under bedroom doors, if closed; or if partially cracked open or all the way open (which is less common than you might imagine: Grandmas have a strange survival instinct; they believe that if a door is mostly closed when an intruder enters the house that the intruder won't see them because the door is closed), it splashes strange, strobic phantasms of infomercials against the hallway floor and wall.

"Boondoggledoggle," *it then tells her.*

Sometimes the TV mutes suddenly. Sometimes there's a rustle of bedsheets and crackling Grandma-joints and the TV remote being fumbled at (sometimes it's on the nightstand, sometimes it's sleeping in the folds of the bed comforter). Sometimes Grandma says:

"Who's there?"

Sometimes the Boondoggle sings, "Boondoggledoggle boondoggle doggle," *and sometimes, if its progressed further in the song, it sings,* "doggle doggle, doggle doggle."

It was this particular Grandma who broke the rules of Grandmas, and while she did have a tweeting hooting chirping fucking wall clock (more Grandmas have these clocks than one might think—and the Boondoggle would know), she also had three mewling offspring—

[*Silence*]

Have you ever hypnotized me, Dr. Oakford?

Because this is how my grandmother, my brother, and my sister died. I've told you this story. But I never wrote this. You actually think this is a—*what?*—a subconscious confession?[5] You're telling me that I wrote these while I was sleeping?

You put a camera in my room and you'll see *what* actually writes these. It's sabotaging me. *IT IS.*

[*Table rattles*]

I was ten years old, Doc. Mom and Dad dropped us off at Grandma's. It was their anniversary; they were having a date night. I will never forget that night and the day leading up to it. My grandmother lived out in the country. My grandfather raised farm animals, but after he died she sold the cows and the chickens and the pigs, too, and all the horses except one. She was old. Massie and *John* (maybe that's why I like you) had played outside most of that day as Grandma watched us on her balcony. She was playing her radio. I remember the gloomy atmosphere—an off-putting, bleak, fatal *genius loci*—and the taking root of a sensation that my ten-year-old brain could not define as Seasonal Affective Disorder. I thought that my strange sadness had caused my brain to play tricks on me. Massie and John—well, they didn't see what I'd seen hiding in the barn loft.

It spoke to me.

It sang that song.

And I chalked it up to my overactive imagination in conjunction to my undiagnosed depression.

I didn't kill my grandmother, Doc; *IT* did; the Boondoggle did.

Are you actually asking me how I know how the Boondoggle kills its victims. You see here? You see the side of my head? That's how I know the Boondoggle used a hammer! You think I did this to myself? You think I killed Grandma, Massie, and John, and then slammed the hammer into my head—not once, not twice, but

---

[5] I do.

thrice? You've taken me as a fool, John.

If you turn off your tape recorder, I'll tell you one thing I've never told you—anyone, in fact—before.[6]

---

[6] The subject tells me that the Boondoggle—despite using a prybar and a hammer—isn't a human at all. He'd never before told me, claims the subject, because it would make him sound crazier. It very well may be that he is unaware that the Boondoggle is a personality of his. But it is peculiar that he is—at least unconsciously—able to differentiate between the other personalities. He knew Daisy had written "Ruby-throated Hummingbirds" because he'd used "them" as their preferred pronoun during his analysis; he knew that Tim had written "Oreos" because Tim is (in the subject's mind, at any rate) a young boy, and had mocked at this; but the "Boondoggle" dream is the only dream that his subconscious mind stubbornly maintained a barrier. Daisy, Tim, and the other personalities were all written in first person; and they all told the murder of the subject's family in different perspectives, in different styles, but with common themes and imagery—and yet the Boondoggle maintains to be referred in the third-perssldfjai

44

II. Great Liminality & Boondoggle

"—STEFANI, you nearly gave me a heart attack."

He took off his headphones.

"I'm sorry, dear, but you've been hunched over your laptop for hours. What are you doing?"

Although his wife's fingers squeezed his shoulders lovingly, he couldn't help but imagine creaturely talons.

"Writing out a transcript of a session I had earlier. Also writing footnotes."

"Is it really *that* important to be up at almost three in the morning?"

"I don't know. Hold on, Stefani; I clicked a few keys when you touched me. Okay, there, I'm done."

She leaned over and started reading.

"You know you shouldn't do that—Doctor-Patient Confidentiality and all that."

"I'm not going to tell anyone—*Blue Jays, Mourning Doves, Cardinals, Crows.* He sure loves talking about birds, doesn't he? He's the schizophrenic, the one who killed himself this morning?"

"No and yes. Not schizophrenia. He had dissociative identity disorder. It used to be called multiple personality disorder, but I suppose it had a derogatory tone, so it was changed. It's commonly confused with schizophrenia. And yes, he killed himself."

"Was he like the guy in the Shyamalan movie?"

"No, but sort of."

"No? Or sort of?"

"Well," said John; he spun his chair to face his wife

and guided her onto his lap. The ceiling groaned. Stefani looked up. Leaves scraped against the window that overlooked the backyard like a dark judgment. John clarified: "There's a personality he didn't quite claim as his own, not in the way he claimed—unconsciously, anyway—the *others*."

"Why does it matter?"

"We think he killed more people. Mind you, he was a minor when he murdered his grandmother and siblings, and it wasn't until he was eighteen years old that his other grandmother—his dad's mother—was murdered in the exact same way. Broken-in window via prybar—and hammer."

"Was there physical evidence?"

"Only circumstantial, but the jury felt it was strong enough. What's the alternative? That an inhuman entity with a fondness of hammers and prybars and grandmothers had followed him for a decade, then sabotaged him by killing his *other* grandmother, conveniently a few months after his grandfather passed? It fits the *modus operandi*. You see, when he killed his grandma and siblings, he took a hammer to his own head."

"Kind of like how he killed himself. Didn't he bash his head against the wall?"

"Yes. And it was likely that *that*—the brain damage via hammer—was the root cause of his disorder. Or maybe he always had it and it made it worse, maybe better. I mean, I'd imagine *something* had to be off in the first place for him to do that to his family. It's hard to say what came first, the chicken or the egg. And my working theory has always been that he might have killed others. This 'Boondoggle' personality might have told me where the bodies are hidden."

"But you don't know and now you'll never know."

"No." John sighed. "I've never spoken to the—

"Listen, why don't you go back to bed. I need to finish up real quick."

"Okay dear. Don't stay up too much longer."

"I won't."

She pecked him on the forehead and crossed his modestly plain office, and when he heard the hallway and bedroom lights click off and the bed springs squeal, he wrote a final thought:

> *What the subject also told me when I turned off the audio recorder was that the Boondoggle visited him frequently, usually around three A.M.—it began after the murder of his family. The Boondoggle threatened that if he told anyone about "its" identity—its quasi-supernatural "inhumanity" (his exact words)—that it would bash in his brains against the wall, and anyone else whom he might tell.*
>
> *I don't know what to make of this.*

John saved his document, closed the laptop, and stretched his back before going to the kitchen for a glass of water. Out the kitchen window the moon was round and huge and cast its moonlight across the expanse of skeletal trees and dead leaves. The term "GREAT LIMINALITY" crept across his mindscape. Gooseflesh followed.

He put the glass in the sink. Picked up junk mail Stefani had left on the pool table and threw it away. Turned off the light. Double-checked the garage door, the front door, and—*yes*—the living room windows: all locked. A photograph of his son, daughter-in-law, and his grandchildren had fallen facedown. Put it back in its stand. Smiled.

"*Hoot hoot—*"

John spun. Heart in his throat. Wall clock chimed

3:00 A.M. Eyes heavy. Nerves jangled. Climbed the stairs slowly. Floor creaked and crackled. In the corner of the high ceiling he noticed the makings of a web and a thick-bodied spider with long legs that almost looked like a—

Crunch.

Under his barefoot on the upstairs landing was a ground-up autumn leaf. It had been such a nice day that Stefani must've opened the window earlier, but why she'd opened the window with a missing screen (it had been on his to-do list to replace it, but he kept pushing it off) was anybody's guess. John picked up five leaves and the crumbles of the one he'd stepped on and threw them away in the bathroom wastebasket.

At the front of the bedroom door was a piece of paper. He bent down and read the words, and then reread the words. Reread them a third time, in fact.

HAMMERHEAD STORK

*They're called—scientifically, at least—*Scopus umbretta, *from the order* Ciconiiformes *(or* Pelecaniformes)*, from the family* Scopidae. *Grandma says that if you take a hammer to a human skull and swing hard enough, it'll break just like the three to six chalky-white eggs which the hammerhead stork lays. I long to see Grandma on the balcony that looks over the* DREAM OF THE GREAT LIMINALITY.

Had Stefani smuggled out another dream journal excerpt? Had she not realized she'd dropped it? Dark implications flooded his brain as he read over the note once more; there were more detailed interpretations of birds that the subject had written in his many decades at the institute, absolutely, but John was almost certain that he'd never written about the Hammerhead stork.

"Stefani?"

He pushed open the door.

Standing over a moveless, dainty, feminine form . . . blots of wine-red decorating the off-white sheet and comforter where a black remote slept in its folds . . . from long pale fingers a hammer drooped loosely, its messy head caked with hair; eggshell; and gray, almosthuman ooze . . . a spectral glow of infomercial washed over what was not a bird . . . outside the window a corroded weathervane spun and sang, "*Boondoggle. Boondoggledoggle.*"

MUSE

"Tell me tales of inconceivable fear and unimaginable love, in orbs whereto our sun is a nameless star, or unto which its rays have never reached."

—CLARK ASHTON SMITH

"I am longing to be with you, and by the sea, where we can talk together freely and build our castles in the air."

—BRAM STOKER, *DRACULA*

"A particularly beautiful woman is a source of terror. As a rule, a beautiful woman is a terrible disappointment."

—CARL JUNG

"No man can describe to another convincingly wherein lies the magic of the woman who ensnares him."

—ALGERNON BLACKWOOD

BORN OF BLOOD
[A LOVE STORY]
—*for Robert Aickman & Thomas Ligotti*

I: *This City is a Vat of Acid*

SAMARA OR SAMANTHA HAS A small scar under her left eye. She's the apotheosis of beauty in a fundamentally flawed way. Her hair is brown. She most certainly has green eyes. Shorter than me but not frail, slender but not sickly, humble but not timid.

Perhaps imagine a point in an obscure primordial darkness when and where a flicker of light, for the first time on this planet or any other planet, came into view, into existence. Just that: a *flicker*. There and gone. But you were there in that distant past, a witness with undeserving eyes, and you leaned over that chasm of chaos below you, where serpents danced, to perhaps listen for some kind of audial evidence of the atemporal impression you thought you saw—you *knew* you saw— where dark had turned bright and dark again. A distorted shape of maybe everything.

Maybe nothing.

And you heard.

Something.

Two promises.

Vague but auspicious.

MY MOTHER AND I WALK at a brisk pace down a colorless corridor with blurred faces and nondistinctive white noise of voices and footfalls around us. At first I don't know where I'm at or why I'm here, and I half-suspect I'm at school and some classmate will whisper, "There goes Jake and *The Sweater Lady*" (my mom always wears sweaters—in fact, she's locally known for it). But I know I'm not in school, I'm thirty-four years old, but every other detail around me is fuzzy with static and it's making me disorientated. I smell sulfur. Suddenly she— not a classmate, but Samara or Samantha—leans out of a room I'm walking past. She's wearing sweatpants or jeans and a modest light pink t-shirt, or maybe it's white, with a pocket in the front. Nothing's in it. Or maybe everything is. Water pools around her feet. And she's got that scar I mentioned; it separates her from the droning manikins around her whose electric voices and ghostly footfalls tickle the peripheral edges of my cognizance. Their crackling joints and obligatorily throbbing heartbeats depress me.

Somehow I know even before she speaks that she's branded *for* me. She's *my* tether. This city is a vat of acid and she's my comfort. Somehow I love her for that. I know all this before she says what she says.

But at first, I admit to you, I don't quite recognize her. Nor do I understand her words. It takes at least five seconds with my neck craning to the point of snapping— assembling with my feeble eyes the form and nature of that flicker of light in that primordial darkness—until I *know* her (but don't necessarily "remember her," if that makes sense) and construct her nine prophetic words: "*Should I give those two gifts that were promised?*"

The veil of abstraction crashes down. I orient myself

to the hospital and the room farther up the corridor where my younger brother lies in a bed of rubber snakes and electronic worms. They crawl out of metal and plastic hovels that protrude with knobs and buttons. They *chirp—*

—chirp—

—chirp—

A symphony of automaton, ethereal crickets.

And then I nod. At first I'm self-conscious as to her misinterpreting my nod for an accidental head movement, perhaps in conjunction with my twisted posture and forward motion. But she herself nods. Understands me. Gives me two thumbs up. The gesture cools down my heart in the fiery blaze of my creeping-onward angst. Then her slender form is gone. Either sucked into the room she'd originally materialized from (the restroom, I realize); or she'd frolicked through the hallway going the other direction, using the droning manikins as cover. She leaves me an impression in my memory of a young woman whose name is most certainly Samara or Samantha. But as I turn back and catch up to my mother, I still can't remember where I'd known her from or what those two "gifts" she'd promised are. I know only that I've known her for as long as I remember—*longer*, maybe—and that the referenced gifts are something beyond my understanding.

A GHOSTLY LIGHT OF DISEASED Jolokia peppers bleeds from an open doorway. We step into the searing glow, *The Sweater Lady* and I (this morning it's an oversized navy turtleneck, the cuffs almost to her knuckles), and look into the open mouth into the throat into the stomach abounding with mundane and quasi-immaterial corrosive agents. There are two manikins dressed as nurses, one as a doctor, but between them—*through* them—I can see a bodily obscenity.

My brother's skin is jaggedly ridged like a Mordorian mountain range. Lesions of lava press up from under patches of white bandage and create dark semicircular spots that look like storm-pregnant thunderheads. "*He's twenty-seven,*" my mother tells the doctor and two nurses, unprompted and unexpected because of the way they jerk and spin, which also causes my brother to turn and look and screech "*ermade ermade ermade*" until the doctor gives him something and he stops and sleeps. And "*how can this happen?*" and "*why does he look like that?*" and "*what did you just give him?*" Then one nurse, faceless and hazy at the edges, is nudged by the doctor-dressed manikin. She moves up the room's gullet toward the rectangular gaping mouth. It's toothless. Because it's a door. But it still gnaws at my numbed existence with its gums. *Sawlike.* Back and forth, and forth and back. It—the room—the scene in the room—the horror in the room—my brother's half-annihilated body in the room—the macabre effigy pulled out from the vat of acid that is this decaying city, this primordial darkness, a chasm teeming with oily chaos serpents in the room—tongues me, lapping off my identity, purpose, *self.* And my mind reaches for that tether, for those two promised gifts. I'm confused because my brother is not a small child, so what gifts could she give that he needs or wants and why don't I remember what Samara or Samantha promised to give him? Maybe the gifts aren't for him after all.

Maybe they're for me.

The nurse pushes us out. What she says sounds like "*you can't see what's not finished,*" my mom says something like "*why was the door opened to begin with,*" but the nurse had already closed the mouth to the cubiform stomach where my brother is being progressively broken down. *Undone.*

My mother and I are staring at the scene through the vertical slit of observation window.

The stomach's lining is thin plaster. Even now—my face inches from the door's closed lips, its *clap* ringing in my ears—I can hear my brother's neighboring patients' wailing and gnashing of teeth.

I want to slam my fist against the faux wood. Show them my badge. Tell them it's police business. But the temptation is a cockroach; it fleets somewhere in my gut where it curls up and dies. Mom tells me to do something I don't at first listen to. Punches my chest for my outward indifference, bunching up her cardigan cuffs in each clenched fist like boxing gloves to buffer the assaults. "*You caught the wrong person!*" she screams accusatorily, and in that moment I think I agree, but then she softens. "*I should never have conceived him, should have aborted him when they told us what was wrong with him, right on the spot, but I was desperate, Jakey, oh so desperate, honey, and now I know you were the only child I was meant to have, and He's taking him back, He's taking him back, his Great Father is, and it's better this way.*"

A crazy urge comes over me to slap her for suggesting—in her irrational, frenzied grief—that no life is better than one with Down syndrome. But I don't. I can't move my hands, anyway. Right now they seem to belong to someone else. So I let her rant. I remain stoic as she strikes my chest a few more times for good measure, like an angry cluster of ellipses at the end of a sentence. She mutters more blasphemy about Kyle's being better off dead. And then she wanders away crying, using one of her bunched-up cardigan cuffs for a makeshift tissue. I watch her. She's an aimless duck quacking in the same pool of acid as her son but just dissolves at a humdrum rate.

I do, too. Dissolve, I mean—not cry, not yet. And if I *do*, I guarantee you I won't sound like a fucking duck getting strangled by wire and bashed against the rocks.

While she goes to the cafeteria, I abscond to the crumbling concrete corridors. I search for the scar on the face that might make sense of this senseless darkness. But I can't remember our mode of contact. I can't even know for certain if her name is Samara or Samantha or something else altogether. As I walk and routinely glance in each and every room, through each and every observation window, down each and every corridor (sometimes getting a whiff of sulfur and concentrated brine), I hunt through my phone's contacts from all my social media platforms for Samara or Samantha or Sam-something, or Sasha, Sarah, Sadie, or Sabrina; comb through direct messages, emails, text messages; scan through deleted or spam folder-assigned messages, as well as recently blocked or disabled accounts; and I find nothing.

SHE'D BEEN THERE, leaning out of that hospital room's mouth, hadn't she? Don't I remember her scar, her voice, her form, her two promised gifts in that primordial darkness? Hadn't I known her name—or a close enough proxy? And I'm about to give my quest to the worms, bury it, and flip a stone overtop, when I happen to cross a room on the third floor. Sulfur again. Briney lights. Lachrymose sufferance.

(*Hoot hoot hoot*)

An old man alone but for a woman-shaped shadow, a pool of water by her feet. His eyes are wide. I see in their gray a hunger for her scar. Her touch. A hunger I desirously share and for no good reason. She bends down open-lipped. I hate the old man as her mouth wraps around his face. His hands, blue-veined and almost translucent, flex and twitch as her mouth opens wider, pythonlike. And her brown hair twists around his wrists to mute his attempted survival.

(*Hoot hoot hoot*)

Churns in and out of timeworn flesh until he's reborn into a knot of death, and then they both fade out through a porthole to a lonely, moon-washed motel for privacy; or they bleed between the stars to the Night Place where, through the crescent of progressively closing manhole cover, comes a gush of saltwater and sulfur and acid—

But none of that happened of course. After an hour or so of looking for Samara or Samantha and finding not a trace of her existence aside from a half-memory, I gather my squawking mother from the cafeteria and drive her home. All the while, she keeps on repeating, "Who would've done that to sweet Kyle?"

"I don't know, mama. I just don't know."

I brake and turn my head. Her face glows yellow, then red. And as I look at her I see, as she wipes away her tears, what looks like a black ink stain on her wrist. She pulls down her cuff again—almost too quickly, too manically—to wipe away her tears, saying:

". . . face, his face, his face, his face, his . . . who would've done *that*, would've done *that* to sweet Kyle, *that* to sweet Kyle? Who who who"

(*hoot hoot hoot*)?

IT'S IN THE MIDDLE OF the night, echoes of a *hoohooing* mother-owl haunting my dreamscape, forming forlorn images of Samara or Samantha and the dying old man, when a hand presses me awake; the sleeves of my mother's nightgown are so long she looks like a great bird. She says, "Jakey, you were screaming, having a nightmare."

I ask if I'd been screaming out the name "Samara" or "Samantha," but I say both names in a sleepy mumble and she doesn't seem to fully comprehend me. She tilts her head at me, blinking. Fearful.

"What did you say?"

"Nothing. Sorry, mama," I say, hugging the Great Mama Bird. She starts crying again (I think somewhere in the sob session she mutters, "*Never say that name again*," although I can't be certain). "We'll catch the bastard," I say. I rub her shoulder. When she finally falls asleep, I go downstairs to the living room where her desktop computer is. I sign on to Facebook and spend two hours clicking through all of my friends' accounts, going through their pictures.

I'm not able to find the young woman with the scar.

But her face and the half-formed memory—maybe even a memory of a memory—is seared—literally seared —into an inaccessible alcove of my brain.

THE NEXT DAY, a Monday, my brother vanished from the hospital. They also say a woman who'd come to see her daughter had vanished, too; all that remained of her were blue jeans and a light pink t-shirt, a picture of her daughter in her shirt pocket.

ON TUESDAY I SEE SAMARA or Samantha standing in the circle of streetlight outside my apartment (my mom's friend Janine said she'd spend a few days with her, so I felt it okay to take a step back into my life). After throwing on a jacket and slippers and bursting out into the quiet little street, the young woman is gone.

Only a bitter impression, a nostalgic afterimage.

And something else. Small, rectangular. In the beacon of streetlight, in a lonely puddle of water, a pupil at its very center. No cars, it's four A.M., but I look both ways before I step into the street and bend down and pick up the photo. It's wet from the puddle but not soaked. I'm dismayed to find that it isn't of Samara or Samantha; but, nonetheless, it's of someone I know— someone I *knew*.

(An obscure, lingering sulfuric scent from somewhere nearby.)

There's no mistaking that the young man in the photo—a school picture, probably Junior or Senior year—is my old partner Charlie Whitman. I can tell by his red hair and dimples and his overall portliness. I guess you might call him *morbidly big-boned*. I'm sure his mama told him so as she shoveled leftover lasagna down his trap. A good detective. A good man, too; maybe too good. At least for the job. Never heard him cuss, not once. He'd have been a better Youth Pastor, but—like I said—a good detective. Competent. Smart enough. Just a little *too nice*. And that used to make me think he wasn't so good, you know? Like he had to have had a cellar full of kids. Not his own, neither. And he never had kids; you know, I think it was because he was too *morbidly big-boned* to do the thing that needed to be done to release unto the world spawn of his own. He'd have been the man I'd want my sons to be, if not for his waist size and my not having any sons. The coroner said he likely had a heart attack while swimming at the local pool. That was four years ago. You ask me, he never seemed like the *swimming-at-the-local-pool* sort of guy, especially not a *sneaking-into-the-local-pool-while-it's-*

61

closed-and-going-for-a-swim sort of guy. Then, when I flip around the photo, I really start to question things. Start to connect the dots between Charlie and my brother Kyle and my mother's accusation from the hospital. Because there's a name on the back—and under it, a weird character. Probably occult.

And as with the unexpected revelation of Charlie Whitman's smiling, pudgy face, the composition of letters on the back of the photo is another blast from the past. But this name brings up a different set of memories, ones tainted and, like a phantom smell but in my mouth, leaves a bad taste on my tongue; I imagine it's how a mixture of shit and battery acid would taste. I spit in the street and actually twist my heel on it—not sure why, I guess it felt right—before stepping back onto the sidewalk and going upstairs and looking in the mirror for a while. Then I power up my dusty MacBook and look up everything to do with who some of the media initially called COP KILLER, but what eventually stuck was THE HOT TUB KILLER. The man who'd been tried and convicted of five accounts of murder, all cops, is Herman Grusenmeyer, and me and Charlie—as you may have deduced—were the ones who caught him six years ago.

It's the name on the back of the photo.

And he's set to be executed in two weeks.

THE VERY NEXT MORNING, the same day the vanished woman's daughter—a six-year-old named Easton Williams died of acute leukemia (they still haven't found the mother, Valora; no leads, either, unless you call me a lead), I call my mother's ex-husband. He used to be my father's partner. The old man is also my mentor.

II: *The Bleeding Between
the Stars*

"WELL?"

The old man sighs.

"Well?"

The old man sighs again and says:

"Well, what? Well water? Wellbeing? Welldoer?"

"Well, what do you think?"

The old man briefly glances at Charlie Whitman on the 4x6 he is holding, hums. Spins it around, soundlessly mouths "Herman Grusenmeyer," nods.

"Well, Nakey-Jakey, what I think is this: I'm retired. And what I want to know is this: why didn't you call this in?"

"Because it's absurd and I'd already fingered the hell out of it. They'd only find my prints. What am I going to say, a lady with a scar on her forehead gave me this photo because she thinks there's a connection and is trying to help? And, because of that, now *I* think there's a connection?"

"Do *you* think there's a connection?" says the old man, lights his pipe, puffs thrice, shakes the match until it bleeds a wispy thread of smoke and places it on his coffee table where displayed across it is a battlefield of blackly dead matches, then he stands and puffs and crosses the room to the window overlooking the old and corroded bones of Shepherdstown.

"There has to be, right?"

"Because of the scarred woman?"

"But you do see why I came to you. The whole thing sounds ridiculous." The old man laughs at this, mutters agreement. I don't blame him. I continue saying, "They'd dismiss it. Say I'm too close. Say my mind's playing tricks because of my brother's condition. Say I'm fabricating a connection between Kyle, Charlie, and *The Hot Tub Killer.*"

The old man sighs and puffs and releases a plume of white-gray. Without looking at me he speaks. "*Well.* Because Kyle was like a son to me when your mom and I . . ." Shakes his head. "Listen, Nakey-Jakey, I suppose it depends on who this lady is. You only *think* you know her name and you *think* you know her—"

"—I *know* I know her—"

"—but you don't know for certain *how* you know her, *where* you know her from, or *when* you first met her. Not to mention the most important: *Why* you know her? Only then will you understand the *who* of the matter. So, okay—she was at the hospital a couple days before your brother disappeared. She was also outside your apartment last night. She left you this . . . *clue*, I guess you could say. And"—he adds this next part cautiously, but also analytically, as if studying my face and mannerisms to make sure what he's about to insinuate *isn't* the case—"this is assuming of course that you're *not* having some sort of . . . mental breakdown." After this moment of face-studying, his own face softens. *Saddens.* "You look like him. Your father. You know, he and I had a similar big case back in our day. It wasn't titled as clickbaity as *The Hot Tub Killer.* But it was gruesome. And it shook our community. I'm certain he never told you about it. And your mother I know for a fact didn't . . ."

"What was the case?"

The old man takes a long drag of his pipe. Holds it

in his esophagus and lungs for five or six seconds before releasing a cancerous stream. He then looks at his pipe, hesitates, sets it on the windowsill. Crosses the apartment and pours himself a coffee ("want some?" "no thanks"). After plopping down on the couch, he takes a conservative sip of coffee, nods, speaks.

"As police, there are essentially three types of humans in the world to navigate. First, there are people who sequentially flush the toilet: these are the law-abiding citizens, typically conscientious, sometimes just shy about it. Maybe they want to expunge the evidence of their shit as if it were a crime. You don't typically have to worry about these people.

"Second, you've got the psycho- and sociopaths; they don't flush. *Period.* He'll leave his deed in a toilet as a . . . I guess you could say 'a grand display of his work.'

"Finally you have the third type. The ones who flush once (maybe they wipe, maybe they don't), close the lid, pull up their pants, fasten their belts (they *always* wear belts), and they may or may not even wash their hands. If you go into a stall and find—you know—bits and pieces of their *you-know-what*, that person is a *bona fide* narcissist, yessir. These pass as normal people because they can always chalk up their one flush as an accident, blame it on the plumbing or something, they were in a rush, or, when they flushed, it all went down but some of it must've crawled back up the pipes to take a swim in the bowl. And because these types pass as normal, they're the—in my opinion—*most* dangerous. They're apt to never get caught if they choose a life of crime.

"You may not have known that your father and I solved the case, but you probably heard the name *Baxter Daniel* floating around town, yeah?"

"Shit, *him.* Didn't they call him *The Baby Killer?*"

The old man laughs. "Not at the time, no. Though I have heard that name circulate in recent years. Probably from the conservative-types. Around election time or something, I don't know. But the media—*prior* to his being caught, of course—called him *The Abortionist*. After he was caught, after the media knew his identity, I think people just called him *a sick fuck*." A humorless laugh, his gray-blue eyes staring at something on the ceiling: a circular stain of moldy abyss leaking from the other side.

"How many women did he kill?" I ask.

The old man, still staring at the abyss-smudge, does the math on his fingers. Doesn't even look at his digits, only at the spot on the ceiling. Does he think that stain will comfort him, tell him what words to say? "Seven," he says, "in the course of three years. All young women. Obviously pregnant. Unmarried. Drugged them up. Killed the late term baby or fetus or whatever you wanna call it. You know how they butcher animals in factories, yeah? Pigs and cows and such? They use this thing, I don't know what it's called, but essentially compressed air pushes out a rod—really, *really* fast. Shoots it into the animal's brain and"—waves an airy, aimless hand—"stuns it, kills it, whatever—and the rod *sucks* back into the nozzle." He scratches his head. "I think it's called a bolt gun. Sounds about right.

"So after drugging up the mother, he would feel around her womb until he found her baby's head and he'd take the bolt gun and—"

"I got it."

"Then he cut the mother open." He makes a movement with his hand as if he'd been the one who'd done it. "She'd still be alive, of course, but wouldn't feel a thing. He'd take the *dead thing* and tie a cord around its—"

"—you don't need to—"

"—and hang it over its mother, from a tree branch or rafter, whatever's available. The coroner thought the mother was still alive when this happened. That's why *The Abortionist*—Baxter Daniel—used extra cord to wrap around her wrists and ankles. Faced her upright, stapled her—"

"—I really don't want to know—"

"—stapled her eyelids open so she could *see*. Sorry.

"The worst thing about it was that your father and I knew him. A lot of people in Shepherdstown knew him. Many liked him because he was a politician-type. Meaning, he was friendly. Talked sports. Prayed for people. Marathon runner. You know, *that* kind of guy."

"But you and Dad, I'm assuming . . . *weren't* fans of him?"

Laughs. "*Yeah*. You could say that. So that had to do with his *less-concealed narcissism* at the same bars your father and I haunted. How to describe the bastard? Let's see. Something like this: Baxter Daniel was the type of guy who masturbated to the stock market; and if that is ever said as a compliment to someone—like they're good with their money, you know . . . *frugal*, whatever—then, well, it wasn't so with Daniel. He was a wealthy man who never showed a charitable bone in his body. Never donated his time or money. But"—he waves a hand—"that's not the characteristic that made us hate him; I'm only illustrating how much of an asshole he was without actually even doing anything. Maybe that's what narcissists are, yeah? Not necessarily *what* they do but what they *don't* do; the absence of good rather than the embodiment of evil—but make no mistake: Daniel ended up being both of those things, but on the surface he appeared only as the former.

"If you look up 'narcissist' in the dictionary, or—

sorry to say because I really, *really* don't like this word—'cunt,' you'll see his picture. Now, I've only used that word maybe five times in my entire life, and four of the five times pertained to describing Baxter Daniel (pre-convicted, I may add). I hate the word. It's degrading. Makes what should be a beautiful thing"—a wink—"into an ugly thing. But I liked that cunt Daniel even less than that word. Damn, Nakey-Jakey, make that six times.

"I'm rambling. I apologize.

"Anyway. He never drank at the bar. Not alcohol, anyway. I think only soda or cranberry juice (something pretentious like that, yeah), but he'd always flirt with the youngest girls—and get this: the fucker was married. The way he openly mingled you'd think they were in an open marriage or something. But no. The 'Godly' man that he was, he claimed he was only witnessing. Spreading the Good News and Lord only knows what else in the category of diseases. Moral of the story, he was a womanizer—not anymore, though, because he got Dahmered with a Bible; ironic, yeah? Some inmate acting as the Left Hand of God bashed in Baxter Daniel's narcissistic brains with a King James after a prison church service, can you believe that?"

Chuckles.

The water stain looks bigger, darker.

A funny smell.

The old man seems so haunted that I wonder if worshiping that black seepage on the ceiling with his eyes is better than thinking of *The Abortionist*. His icy irises inflamed, with wormy veins invading the white around them—are brittle as they jitter. Somehow he finds the will to look away from the void. He finds my eyes.

"But his waterhole-womanizing was not the worst of it.

"In my time as detective, over the course of six or seven years, *a goodly portion* of his foreign exchange students had filed charges against him. There was never any physical evidence, and more than a few members of the school board were chummy with him, so all he received was a slap on the wrist. And the girls—always girls, usually Norwegian blondes (sometimes he'd throw in a brunette for variety), always tall and thin and long-legged—well, they just went to other homes and they received generous sums of money to zip it. It's always like that, isn't it? Dahmer and Bundy. So many red flags. It's usually cops looking the other way, or sometimes it's just the limitations of the law. Testimony is rarely ever good enough, and the Norwegian girls—after their gifts of hush-money—never advanced their allegations. Until the trial, of course. Three of the five girls flew in from their home countries to testify against him.

"That's why your father and I hated his guts, even before our finding the smoking gun that he was *The Abortionist.*"

I sit there for a moment.

"What was the smoking gun?"

He hesitates, looks at his pipe, looks at the spot on the ceiling, looks at me.

"Well, there's no such thing as a perfect person and there's no such thing as a perfect killer. You may have known via gossip-osmosis that the final victim wasn't a successful fatality. He drugged her up like normal, killed the baby like normal, did the sick fucking ritual like normal—if you can even call any of that *normal.* But what he didn't know, because he wasn't actually a doctor of course, was that there were twins in the mother's womb. He'd only killed one. We're not exactly sure if the other baby started crying, that she—the baby—was making too much noise, so he just fled. Or if she started crying later, which got the attention of a neighbor, which allowed the ambulance to come at a timely fashion; I hate imagining the latter scenario; the girl barely survived and she's lucky she didn't have brain damage from being hooked up to a half-dead battery—forgive the analogy."

"Why are you telling me all this?" I ask him, to which he tilts up his head again as if an invisible string is attached to his chin, as if something in the moldy spot— the thing staring back at him—is tugging ever so gently. Nudging his attention back to the black.

"Why?" the old man says to the abyss. Blinks like a dumb cow. "I . . . you asked, didn't you?"

"I'm here about Kyle, Old Man. The Charlie-Herman connection. The photograph. The girl."

"*The girl*," the old man murmurs. Blinks again. A luminosity possesses his pre-cataract eyes. "The *girl*, something about the girl, the mother, the girl, the scar." He rubs his chin, and I wonder if he's unconsciously feeling for the hook the abyss-tugging string is attached to; he mutters something about their "can't be a connection . . ." and ". . . be right back, Nakey-Jakey."

The old man sips his coffee and then stands. His joints crackle like the snapping sap of slow-burning wood. Hobbles to a cabinet against the wall and opens a drawer and starts fingering through folders.

"Why do you call me that?" I press while he's busy doing what he's doing. "Nakey-Jakey."

"Why do you call me 'Old Man?'"

"I don't know. Because you were older than Dad by—what?—fifteen years. You had gray hair ever since I can remember. A lot older than Mom when you, um, married her."

Distractedly he says, "It didn't last long, you know— your mother and me." He stops digging through the drawer and stands straight and laughs and says without turning, "I swore she just wanted to get married so I could adopt you boys and change your last names to *Fischer*. Like she wanted to get rid of his last name, yeah? Reminders, maybe? We never even, you know—"

"—you're right, I don't want to know."

"Well, we didn't. Hell, she wouldn't even take off her sweatshirts." A laugh. "Always long sleeves. Shit, I forgot what you asked."

"Nakey-Jakey."

"Oh. Yes. After the playground incident—"

"—playground incident?"

Now I look at the spot on the ceiling; it reminds me of something, a lost memory.

"Nothing. I don't know," he says too quickly. "Something spooked you; I wasn't there; if you don't remember, then don't worry. Anyway. You used to always want to take baths when you were a kid. Three or four times a day, if you could. We thought maybe it was a . . . *quirk*. Used to strip down so frequently that whenever I came over to your house—when your dad was alive, that is—I'd often see a naked little boy dart across the hallway, either headed to the bath or from." He shrugs and turns back to the drawer and gets busy searching for something. "I started calling you 'Nakey-Jakey,' and I guess it stuck like a noodle on the wall."

"Weird. I don't remember any of that," I say, and I really don't. Nothing about the playground, nothing about excessive bath-taking.

"Don't worry; I don't even remember what I ate this morn—"

The old man becomes rigid.

"What is it?" I say.

"Her name, the mother's, coincidence surely . . ." says the old man, hands on a sheet of paper—a

71

newspaper cutout, I can make out. "I don't believe in the supernatural, Nakey-Jakey."

"*Samina.*" The name flows out like gospel. It's as if I'm reading the caption from his eyes.

I stand.

I cross the apartment.

"Coincidence," says the old man, then he starts guarding the newspaper cutout.

My feet are slow and light. The room spins.

"Where can I find her?"

"*Jake*, listen to yourself. It's just a coincidence. It's not like this case is related. I was just illustrating to you that Herman Grusenmeyer is a sick fuck and deserves to be lethally injected. You caught a filthy human. Charlie was not murdered by *The Hot Tub Killer*. Your brother was . . . *I don't know*. There's no connection here. If anything, your mystery scar-lady is the killer and she's definitely not Samina Redman."

I stand behind the old man. I see a hand—it's mine—reach over his shoulder and grasp the newspaper cutout ("Don't," he nearly shouts, so now I

[*am sitting on a bench, a comic book on my lap,* Fantastic Four, *a woman approaching*]

must). Now it's in front of my face. The woman is young; the apotheosis of beauty; brown hair; shorter than me but not frail; slender but not sickly; and if the photograph had been in color, she may have had green eyes; but she has no scar, and—despite a vague resemblance—the old man is right. It is not *my* Samina.

"If you really want to find her, I know what cemetery she's buried in. You *really* don't remember, do you?"

"Remember what?"

He waves a hand, flustered, nervous. "Never mind. But anyway, you could have just as easily turned in this mystery photo to the station. Or held onto it. Or I could just as easily have talked about something else or refused to help—because, well, like I said: *I'm retired, Jake*—and I know you love your brother, Lord knows he was like a son to me during that period of time—but Jake, if you think this girl knows anything about your brother's disappearance, anything at all, it *needs* to go through the proper channels. But more likely than not, some sicko with a propensity for hurting mentally handicapped people is who you are looking for."

"You're wrong," I tell him, my eyes darting around the newspaper cutout. I'm looking at the words but not reading them. Looking at the mother but not seeing her. Looking at the baby, the baby girl, the girl. "There's a connection. Do you know why I came to see *you* and not anyone else?"

The old man turns and shrugs and sighs. "Because I'm the closest thing to Sherlock Holmes. I don't know. You tell me."

I study his face. My hand reaches out and caresses his strange, almost alien skin. It's rubbery and cold. Like a Halloween mask. And for a second I actually think that it is. And I wonder who he is. And where I am. When I am, how I am. Outside the apartment's window, from the street, I hear a

(*hoot hoot hoot*)

radio gushing out from a car that will soon be a time-molested rust can, if it isn't already, because this city is a vat of acid and the only light we can ever hope for is that which bleeds blackly onto our planet from some source between the stars, from somewhere very cold and very dark; and as I hear the *hoot hoot hooting* and the almost inaudible crepitation of this city's moldering bones, I look away from the newspaper cutout, away from the old man's gristly peel, and I look at what had lain underneath the ink-stained tree shaving in my fingers—a photo. Some divine sleight of hand, some arcane kismet that may have literally been placed in the deck before I was born. I see her kiss his old man lips, see her mouth open wide, her hair intimately consume him, romantically twist around him, devour him; a perfect consummation of life and death.

"I dreamed that you *knew* her, that you loved her too. And you *do*. I see that this isn't random."

"Know *who*, love *who*?" Confused.

"The girl." I nod forward.

"*Who*?" He turns, looks around even more confused than a second ago; maybe a little scared, too. "You're not making sense, Jake."

"Her."

"Her?" Now he sees. He picks up the next photo in the drawer, a senior-year photo. She's got brown hair, green eyes, thin but not sickly, and she's the most beautiful girl I've ever seen. I mentally add about six or seven years and a scar; without a doubt, she's the girl who stepped out from that hospital room and spoke of promises to keep.

"Her," I repeat and I find my hand snatching the photo. "I know her."

"Well," says the old man, "I'll tell you one thing, buckeroo: she wasn't named after her mother. Name's Maggie, not Samina."

I know I sound like a broken record, but I can't help but say it one more time. "I know her."

III: *That Which Stares Back
From Somewhere Very Cold
and Very Dark*

AUSPICIOUS SCENTS OF VAGUE FLOWERS and sweet
seawater ride gales over the sandy beach where her
house stands, a lighthouse on a tall ridge looming over
at a distance no less than half a mile but may as well
have been a toy-sized building on a mound of sand
directly behind it. The two promises she'd given me,
something I can't remember—nor, if this makes sense,
something I never knew to begin with—orbit around my
head. Metaphysical satellites whining, buzzing.

As I step out of my white Toyota, feeling a strange
sensation accentuated after having discovered the girl's
name is Maggie instead of Samara or Samantha or
Samina and lives a couple states away in New Jersey, I
hear something—a seagull—and turn to face my car. I'm
afraid I won't find it again for the way the too-white sand
had invasively crawled upon the blacktop, smothering
the surface.

Then I turn and look at the address number on a
board nailed to a tree. The numbers are made of shells.
I compare it to the ripped-out sheet of lined paper the
old man had given me. It's the right address, it's the
right house.

Maybe everything I've been looking for awaits me
here. I must move closer, find answers. As I walk, the
sun blinks out, shines again, blinks out. The sand

slithers and I think of fighting serpents. And if I am to dig there or there or there, would I find a chaotic chasm, one nearly endless? A festering wet hole I'm not meant to see? If I were to dig and dig and peer through the hole deep beneath the sand and the fucking serpents, would I find myself looking over, from a bird's-eye view, a thirty-five-year-old man who looks exactly like me seated across from an old man who looks exactly like the old man in my dream, where he was kissed by Maggie or Samina, in an apartment overlooking the antediluvian bones of Shepherdstown? Would I rehear the tale of *The Abortionist* and his last victim, Samina, and the born-dead baby girl and the other girl who survived—Maggie— the one born of blood? Would I see the thirty-five-year-old man who looks exactly like me follow the old man to his filing cabinet and reach over his shoulder and—

The sun is swallowed by deep, dim thunderheads. It's sunless but somehow the glass of the lantern room of the lighthouse reflects some obscure light. The shadowiness of the sand, how it looks dark brown instead of white, casts forth from my imagination a primordial world and—

There before me, a light. Still too far away to see the scar. She's standing before the beach house on the side yard. A shovel in one hand, the other hand shielding her eyes (from what, I don't know; the sun is still gone, and she's the only light, the *first* light) as she stands looking toward me, studying the man ambling toward her.

A look of recognition?

I step onto the path of laid, mottled brick—which seems to reach around the entire house, including the area in which she stands—and when I'm close enough she takes down her hand and says melodiously but timidly:

"Can I help you, sir?"

It's her voice, I manage to think between galloping heartbeats.

Through her summer dress I can see her form is verily slender but not sickly-thin. Certainly not. Not frail, for there seems to be imbued about her an athleticism, but shorter than me by at least a foot.

Closer now, I see her green eyes cut through the blackened world around us. Her hair is brunette, too, but I'd been wrong about something. Two things, really:

Firstly, she's the apotheosis of beauty in a fundamentally flawless way. That's because of the second reason. She doesn't have a scar.

Even though I know her name is Maggie, *apparently*, I still have to make sure. Ten feet from her, I say, "Samina?"

At first she's confused, then edgy. Looks me up and down. A look in her emerald eyes as she studies my face, my body, my clothes. A squall of wind screams across the beach from an oncoming storm that I hope to avoid. For a moment her hair—similar to that which wrapped around and implanted their tips into the flesh of the old man in my dream, until he'd been a knot of death—is a living thing, wild and wicked, and using her free hand that is much tanner than *my* Samina's (somehow I always thought she originated from somewhere cold and dark, like Alaska), she tames the unruly hair. But the wind doesn't settle, and her bangs are still thrashing. It *had* been a look of recognition; I see that now as her lips—similar to those which stretched across the old man's face in my dream, until they both faded out—say something that confirms this.

They say my name.

"Jake?"

Then:

"Jake Sullivan?"

AFTER SHE INVITES ME INSIDE and pours me a cup of coffee she'd already made, we dissect a bit more the matter of our partial correctness in each other's names. She *is* Maggie Redman *not* Samina: that is—*was*—her mother's name. I *am* Jake Fischer *not* Jake Sullivan: that is—*was*—my father's name. I told her about the old man who married my mother and who adopted me a few months after my father's death; about how Marge, Jake, and Kyle Sullivan had then become the Fischers.

"That's strange, isn't it?" she says.

"All of it is," I say.

"No," she says, "none of it is as strange as *that*." (I wonder what her definition of "strange" is, since I strongly disagree, but I let her continue.) "It would be one thing if she and your stepfather—"

"—they divorced," I say. "He's just . . ." I shrug. "An old man, now."

"Okay. It would be one thing if maybe they *did* create a bond in the mourning of your father and fell in love and got married and by way of respecting the traditional ways of marriage—assuming your mother isn't a popular actress or singer whose name provides her a considerable income—she wanted his name and to give his name to her children, which is you and your brother. But you said that she divorced him immediately after they got married. And neither of them were too upset about it. Why?"

"I listen, Damina—I'm sorry, I mean *Muggle*—I don't know. I was a kid. The real mystery is how'd you know my father? And how'd I know what you looked like without ever having met you?"

"My mother *did* look like me and your father *did* look like you. Maybe you just remember her."

"I never met her."

"Are you sure about that, Jake Fischer?"

I stutter for about fifteen seconds until she steers the conversation—as if this is an intellectual tug-o-war—back to my family.

"How did your father die?"

"He drowned," I say. "Got drunk, took a bath. Fell asleep. Turned on the faucet by mistake, or so they think. Extra hot. Had sores all over his body, burns . . ."

. . . and then I think of Charlie, who never seemed like the swimming-at-the-local-pool sort of guy . . .

. . . and I think of my brother, who'd been found with such severe burns that the doctors only *assumed* it was acid of some sort. The forensic lab had yet to identify anything definitive.

Could there be a *deeper* connection? There is no way it's *The Hot Tub Killer,* Herman Grusenmeyer; he'd been in prison when Charlie had died and is *still* in prison; and there was no way he had killed my father, because he wasn't born yet.

I pull out from my pocket the photograph. I look at Charlie's face, Herman's name, the symbol.

Out loud I say, "Then who gave me this? And why?"

My voice is far away. So is she: distorted and long. She says something. What does she say?

Outside, thunder clambers across the firmament between sea and heavens. Rain starts pattering against the sides of the beach house. I look across the too-large living room. Decorating the tops of the cabinets and dressers and shelves are small, strange, simple dolls. Buttons for eyes. Lifelike hair. Waterlogged and corroded appearances, as if they'd been retrieved from a city teeming to its rim with acid; dark stains bleeding between the stars via patches of black and gray discoloration; and a moldy abyss leaking from the other side, which stares back—they *all* stare back—at me from somewhere cold and dark, from some consecrated void where a Forlorn Thing cries alone. So very cold—so very dark—the Night Place is—a moonlit motel on the lonely highway in the black decay in the sky. I shiver and look back at her stringy form. Then at the black eye in my mug I gaze, transfixed, paralyzed—its pupil reflecting my face. My hand reaches up. My fingers stretch out and twirl across the room where they entwine the area with fleshy web.

And the young woman with the scar stands behind Maggie, pale and dripping

(*acid*)

water.

They're identical if not for the scar. They're identical if not for the death.

As I drain backward through my chair and into the floor and the sand and the chaos realm of dancing serpents—

—THE PERFECT BLACK PRAYS FOR stars and suns; famished abyss hungers for slop and chum; apotheotic beauty has a scar I love; and the consecrated void is a lonely god.

Perfect abyss, apotheotic void: that which stares back from the acid between the—

"*Stars slop scar god,*

   "*stars slop scar god,*

      "*stars slop scar*—"

A forlorn god.

"*Of blood*—"

—A CHARCOAL-BLACK SONG PLAYS out to me. It's impreg-
nated with a charnel rot. The cold, somewhere beneath
me (it's too dark to move), expunges—at least temporarily—ugly atrocities from far above and way beyond: the
unholy offspring of misery. Through the words, through
the stench, comes a girl, a scar. A promise. A light and
a darkness. And another light—milky at first, and then
somehow *sizzly* like butter in a skillet. A fidgety outline
surging with crucial descriptions, and then those descriptions—those *definitions*, flickering tongues of chaos
in void—dislodge from its

(*sister*)

mother lode, and even those specks, spinning discs
of fiery color and sound and scent, sputter and dissolve
and reform.

Then a cawing mêlée of crows; a song of a mad,
spiraling murder; of wings and feathers and beaks calling squawking howling—

"*Jakey?*

"*Jakey?*

"*Jake, can you hear me?*"

I suppose technically I hear something—although
I'm momentarily agnostic to the meaning and existence
of "me" in me or anyone or -thing else. I'm able to use
my fingers that somehow are solid and compact (they're
not long and jointless *Twizzlers* as one might expect
after being stretched around a room

where room

when room

why room

several times over) to feel the substance about the
ground where I lay. It's cold cement. And some*thing* else.
A hard rectangular *thing*. It's not a frenzied murder of
crows; it's my mother speaking to me, marginally
vibrating. "*Jake,*" it says. "*Listen very carefully, Jake,*" it

81

says. "*Remember the other night,*" it says, maternal and somehow familiar, but an unsettling static sutures through the words, making them sound garbled and fuzzy just like the form I'd seen that is now a vague dream upon waking, one that I can't *quite* remember. All there is is the voice. The rectangular cold shape, too. My fingers fumble with it; they might as well be *Twizzlers* on account of their rubbery uselessness.

"Mom?" My voice is far away and melted. Indefinite and wretched.

"*Yes honey, yes. Where are you?*"

In a vat of acid, I think but hold my tongue as not to panic the woman who'd birthed me.

"I'm away," I think I say.

"*What are you doing?*" An edginess in her voice. A concern.

Bleeding between the stars, I open my mouth to say mordantly but can't prove that I'm not, and that uncertainness unnerves me. Because I don't want to jinx myself, I instead say:

"Driving. You're on speaker phone" (she isn't). "I'm listening" (sort of). My breath, what with black noise and a living rot, comes with difficulty. I strain every molecule of my body and soul to listen to her dark-strangled voice.

"*Remember the other night,*" she repeats, "*when you were having that nightmare. At first I didn't think anything of it. Thought it was gibberish. You know how it is when people sleep talk. Never quite makes sense, does it? One time, when you were a kid, you kept on repeating you'd left the pencils in the freezer. So I thought that's what it was: meaninglessness.*

"*But based on what Frank told me*" (sometimes I forget the old man has a name) . . . She sighs. "*That you came over to his apartment in a tizzy, regarding a photo and a lady and your brother and . . .* serial killers.

"*Oh Jakey.*

"*You can hear me, can't you?*"

"Yes, mama," wrings out my mouth.

"*You're glad you were born, aren't you? That you exist?*"

"What kind of question is that?" I'm more alert now and twice as confused.

"*You sound so far away, honey,*" she says. Sighs. "*You used to play with* things *when you were a kid. It was odd. Even as a baby, you'd ogle and coo at one particular corner in the nursery. Your father—forgive him, Jakey—well, he thought you were retarded; ironic, really, considering your brother's condition. But I knew you weren't; and I suspected I knew why you acted that way, but never told anyone—I couldn't. Other people suggested imaginary friends.*

"'*As a baby?' I'd counter, and nobody would have a good explanation. Then one day I was sweeping the wood floor in the nursery and I went to move your crib so I could get underneath. It fell over—don't worry, you were downstairs playing. And that's when I saw that sketched into the bottom of the crib—with what looked like a faded black marker—was something I'd never seen before. It looked like witchcraft to me.* Satanic.

"*I bought you a new crib. And guess what, Jakey?*"

"I stopped talking to *things*," I say. It was an instinctive response and my mom's confused, uneasy silence is frightening as much as it's humorous.

"*Well, no,*" she says after a spell, "*your father's being a policeman had some perks. I sketched the symbol on a piece of paper before burning it and took it into the station and told your father about what happened and where I'd found the symbol. And he looked pale. Very pale, like he either knew what it meant. Or was guilty about something. And I asked him, I said, 'Jake Sullivan'—so*

83

he knew I meant business—'what in God's name does this mean?'

"*He even had the gall to ask if I was certain that I already didn't know! Can you believe that, Jake? How would I know what it meant?*

"*Anyway. He took the occult symbol and went back into his cubical. Picked up the phone and called someone. I had the romanticized notion that he was calling a pagan symbols expert from Harvard or something, but it became pretty obvious when he came back that the phone call hadn't been to a professor but* had *been about the symbol all the same.*

"*All he told me was, 'It won't happen again,' and, Jakey, guess what? It didn't. What I mean is: it didn't stop. You continued to ogle and coo at the nothingness in the corners of the rooms or dark water stains on the ceilings . . .*"

. . . footfalls, crackling thunder, raindrops; I think I'm in the lady-without-the-scar's basement . . .

"*. . . when you were a bit older, you called these imaginary friends 'orphans,' and I'd ask if they were children, but you never answered. More sense came from this when I found out to whom Jake had sat down and called in his cubical that day years earlier, and* why *he called. When she knew that I knew, that's when the day at the playground happened. Then after that day, Jakey, you became friends with a girl that was nine months older than you, a girl with a scar.*"

Gooseflesh explode across my flesh.

"*But I didn't know about the girl until later.*"

Samina.

My voice sliding on sandpaper, I ask, "What the fuck happened on the playground and why can't I remember it?"

Footfalls, a door creaking open, a silent petite

silhouette at an odd angle from where I lay. I want to question my mother like she's in the box, but my mouth becomes rigid. A pathetic whistling through my nose. Where her eyes are are green flickers of candlelight, starlight-glistening emeralds, or darkness-penetrating jadestone. And above her, at the top of the stairs, a disc like an open manhole floating above her. Water dripping out. What looks like hair—no, what *is* hair—and then a pale face half-revealed by the open doorway behind her—*its*—living, breathing twin—and then the legs of a crab scuttling out—a hand with too many joints, fingers elongated, and jagged, overgrown nails—and then an arm, too-long, and hemorrhaging from its skin moon-shine and acid—and then my mother's voice:

"*Jake?*

"*Jake?*

"*Jake, can you*

CLOSE YOUR EYES AND LISTEN to this ticking sound. I want you to let go of all the tension in your body—your neck and shoulders, your hands and feet, and your face—and breathe normally as you might consider going to your favorite spot. There's a light rain or a mild wind. It's not hot outside, wherever you decide to visit; but neither is it cold; it's just right, like the porridge in that bear story.

"*From this point onward, I want you to dig really deep, Jake. Remember every detail. Okay. Let's begin.*

"*Are you reading a comic book?*"

"*Yes.*"

"*And now someone visits you. She must be a kind woman. You like her, don't you? That's why you talk to her, right? Can you tell me what she looks like?*"

"*I'm at the playground where Tommy and I some-times go to play ninjas on the monkey bars. I'm reading a comic book. I can't remember the issue but for some reason I'm being impatient because there's no villain yet, no monster, and I've been reading for a while now. I'm almost at the end. There's still nothing. He or it—or she— is in the world somewhere but I don't know them. They're hiding between the words. Between worlds. But there's hope in there, because I know it's not a hopeless cause to know them, even though I don't see them. And I hear something. A woman's voice, so I look up."*

"*What does she say?*"

"*'Jake Sullivan.' My name. And at first I think she's a teacher. One of my elementary teachers. A younger one. Pretty. But I don't say anything yet because—even if she is a teacher and knows my name—I don't know her and don't know her name. And she has something in her hand. It's a white rag. She says that she's sorry but my dad chose this.*"

"*Does she say what your father chose?*"

"*I don't know. She says a poem.*"

"*A poem?*"

"*She's got promises to keep and miles to go before she sleeps. Miles and miles to go. And she starts crying, so I set my comic book down and ask her if she's okay.*"

"*You never answered my question: What does she look like?*"

"*Brown hair, green eyes. A little shorter and thinner than Mom, but not frail or sickly-looking. Her eyes have ghosts in them.*"

"*What do you mean, Jake?*"

"*They're haunted.*"

"*Is she alone?*"

"*Yes. Wait. No. The lady sits down next to me. A woman walks her dog so the lady beside me doesn't look as crazy as she did a moment ago—*"

"*What do you do mean by 'crazy'?*"

"Her face is weird. Contorted. Like her expressions don't fit under her skin."

"And then what happens?"

"She puts what I initially think is a handkerchief or a tissue paper back in her pocket. She whispers to me. She says, 'This city is a vat of acid, it killed my girl, and your father won't clean it out.'

"I ask her if that's how she knows my name, through my dad, because we have the same name. And she nods and blinks away tears. She says, 'That's right. Right before you were conceived, my daughter got—she got bit by a dog. That's why she has a scar right there. No, don't look at her. She's not complete yet; even after I do what I'm about to do (please don't scream), she'll only be a fraction . . . an impression, an afterimage . . . of her full potential. It may take years before you can truly see her, feel her. Look at me, Jake. That's a good boy. I told your father about the dog that bit my daughter, who did that to her face, and your father, he showed me pictures of men—I mean, dogs—and asked me if I knew any of them. I said I did. That one and that one.

"'At this point he looks at his partner. You see, there's a mean ol' Rottweiler in town. One that barks at the girls. That dog's barked at me a few times, too. Mean ol' dog, needs to get his balls remo—I mean, he needs to get fixed. Your father doesn't like this Rottweiler named Baxter and he's already decided it's the one that bit me and my daughter.'

"She looks up at the trees and I follow her eyes. There's a black spot above them but below the sky. It's weird-looking, like an optical illusion. It's too low, too colorful. It's daytime, it has to be, but I see the stars. Strange constellations. The Little and Big Dippers have dipped into the wrong stuff. There are living things bleeding between the stars. At first I think I'm dreaming

87

it. There's something inside."

"What's inside it?"

"Something. Is staring. At me. From that. That blackness, oh, OH GOD, IT HAS A DEAD YELLOW EYE, A LIGHTLESS SUN, AND THE ORPHANS THE ORPHANS THE ORPHANS, THEY'RE CRYING OUT AND LEAKING OUT AND SALTY AND WET LIKE TEARS! DADDY DADDY DADDY DADDY!"

[mommy's right here Jakey]

[it's okay   I have it under control   please remain quiet and unobserved Mrs. Fischer . . .]

". . . now, Jake, everything is okay. Relax. Breathe; good; breathe in . . . and out. Very good. Look away from the sky for now; it's a false memory—meaning, it never happened. What does the woman do?"

"She grabs my chin and turns my face so I look into her green eyes, because I think she knows what I'm seeing; she's doing the same thing you're doing; doesn't want me to dwell on the Night Place. It scares me. Because I suddenly don't think it's my imagination anymore. Also, I don't think the pale girl that I'd seen hiding behind the lady was in my head, I think she's like one of the Orphans."

"Jake, what do you mean by 'Orphan'?"

[his imaginary friends]

[let him talk . . .]

". . . Jake, can you answer me? Who are the Orphans to you?"

"They're lost and they don't have parents anymore."

"Jake, can you tell me where they come from?"

"They leak out from the Night Place."

"Thank you for elaborating, Jake. Now let's get back to the lady; does she reach for the handkerchief?"

"No, because now kids come. I think they must be homeschooled because I don't know them. I don't know why them coming to the playground makes her not want to wipe away her eyes. But she doesn't, even though I know she wants to because she's crying. She still has her hand under my chin. Her eyes look crazy again. Contorted. I think she might bite me like that Baxter-dog.

"She says something else. 'I told your dad that the dog's paws were manicured. Pink nails. I told him that the dog had a daintiness about it. Not a Rottweiler but maybe a small Collie. A girl dog. With a tattoo, a scary tattoo, an evil one; Baxter doesn't have any. But your dad doesn't like this answer. He tells me that Baxter has done some really terrible things; bitten lots of girls; "and if you don't testify against him," your dad tells me, "then you will be an accomplice."'

"'An accomplice?' I ask.

"'Yes,' she says. 'For when the Baxter-dog forces itself upon another girl-dog, making her pregnant. Maybe even killing her. Then it would be my fault. That's what your dad told me. And you know what, Jake Sullivan?'

"'What?' I say.

"'I don't disagree. So I point at that narcissistic dog Baxter. I nod. And you know what I tell your father and that old partner of his?'

"I shake my head no.

"'I tell them I'll agree as long as they understand that the killer will think she is getting off scot-free. That the dog that bit my stomach'—she lifts up her shirt and shows me; a kid nearby sees her scar, or maybe the bottom of her breasts, and says the f-word—'and the dog that bit my daughter, disfigured her face for eternity, is going to celebrate when she reads in the news that The Abortionist got caught and he's a real sick'—now she says the f-word—'and do you know what an M.O. means?'

"I shake my head no.

"'Modus Operandi. *It's a Latin term. Has to do with the pattern in which the dog chooses* which *people to bite, and* how *to bite them,* when *to bite them, and* why. *And looking at you, and looking at your brother, I* think *I know why. Shh, no questions; just listen: Like I said, Jake, I told your father and his old man partner that I'll agree because I did know that Baxte*r'—another f-word, sorry— 'and he did growl at me a few times and he did need to be stopped, because your dad and his partner were right—that dog was a ticking time bomb. But I promised them something. Two things. An eye for eye. On that hospital bed I swore to the Creator that if the real biter was never brought to justice, that what was done to my baby girl will be done in similar fashion to his future children. I cut my hand, Jake, and your father cut his— reluctantly, sure, but I made him—and he shook my hand and the deal was done.'*

"*I tell her I don't want to be bit.*

"*She laughs. Cries. Says, 'No one knows the hour or the day that you'll get bit. But I came here today to let you know that when the hour and day comes, you can blame your daddy.'*

"'*What if my dad finds the dog?' I ask.*

"'*Then you tell him, when you get home, that he needs to hurry the "f-word" up . . .'*"

Silence.

"Jake? Can you tell me what happened next?"

Silence.

"*She introduced me to her daughter. The pale girl was from somewhere very cold and very dark and wet; I thought she was a mermaid until recently. I think she came from that spot above the trees which bled between the stars. But I don't think she was that which stared— which* still *stares—back; I think that's my Fa—*"

[my son does *not* see or talk to dead people   my son

90

is a normal boy—]

[Mrs. Fischer why don't you go sit in the waiting room   it must be terribly warm in here wearing that sweater   it's cooler out there . . .]

". . . *Jake, do you remember the daughter's name?*"

"*Samina.*"

"*You seem certain.*"

"*I am certain. She's my best friend and . . . well, I guess she's the only Orphan that kinda looks like me.*"

"*How does she look like you, Jake?*"

"*She looks human.*"

"*The others don't?*"

"*The others look more like Fa—*"

[—enough of this   I want my son to forget all about this witch and her demon daughter and all these fucking Orphans]

[I'm getting there Mrs. Fischer   if you'd let me finish   we are making great progress today   but before he forgets he needs to remember as much as possible   that way we can put this episode in a box and bury that box deep in his subconscious mind   shall I . . . ?]

"*Jake, I want you to continue telling me about what the woman at the playground did. I know this part is scary, but you'll feel better releasing it. Okay?*"

"*Okay. She puts a hand on my head so I can't move. With her other hand she pulls out what I now realize is a cloth that is wrapped around a knife. She grabs the knife and the cloth falls and flies away and I think she's going to use it on me. To bite me. She says something in another language. Sounds like she's praying. Something is coming down from the spot above the trees. I want to turn my head and see what it is—try to—but the woman's hand is strong and I can't. I only see out the side of my eyes some black shape like a . . . squid or jellyfish. Something from the abyss. It's black though, whatever it is, and I see*"

91

Samina's face. For the first time. She's standing behind her mother, her chin on her shoulder; they look like Siamese twins blending into one. And I know I love her; I know she's my . . . my tether. *She has a small scar under her left eye from where the dog bit her. She's beautiful. Her hair is brown. She has green eyes like her mother. Shorter than me but not frail, slender but not sickly, humble but not timid.*

"I think she's the Light God talked about before the sun was made. This one teacher talked about how that debunked the Creation story, because how could light exist before the sun? But I don't think he'd ever met her: the First Light that hovered over the abyss. The one that defined Good and Evil, Day and Night. She's only there for a moment in that primordial darkness. Just a flicker. There and gone. There *as her mother takes the knife, puts it to her own throat, and slices; then* gone *after the blood rushes into Samina's mouth—she's thirsty, she hasn't drunk for years, this is the First Light's first meal. And when she fades back into one of the stars, where the Orphans of the . . . the* ATERCOSM, *yeah, that's what they call it, yeah, that's where they come from and where they go back to—a motel on a long, lonely highway, no cars in its parking lot, and a lightless moon always watches over—I can still see a residue, the spot where she'd been hunched over her mother—*

"Then someone screams. And I remember waking up in the hospital room. Samina is back. She'd been talking to me while I slept."

"What did she say to you?"

"I—I can't remember.

"Something about . . .

"Two promises . . .

"Vague but good."

"Jake, this girl is not real. Samina Redman was the

woman who killed herself sitting next to you on the bench. Her daughter, the one with the scar, must be your guilt manifested as the daughter that had been killed by Baxter Daniel, The Abortionist. *You've heard stories about him at school, and you recognize the name and— even though it's been years and you hadn't been born at the time of the killings—you must also recognize the woman, because she was the only survivor. A local once-celebrity. When she's talking about the dog biting her and her daughter, you imagine the daughter having a scar. But she was never bit by a dog, Jake. And she died before she was even truly born. The girl you claim is your friend was never alive.*

"*So when you hear the snap of my fingers, you won't remember Samina anymore. You will put this trauma in a box, find a room somewhere in your head (a bedroom, a library, whatever you choose—there are no limits), and shove it behind something. Maybe find some loose floor-boards, pry them out, put the Samina-Box down there, put the boards back on.*

"*Have you done that, Jake?*"

[*A beat*]

"*Yes.*"

[*Snap*]

IV: *The Consecrated Void is a Lonely God*

FIRST THERE WAS DARKNESS, then a light. Across what my drug-addled brain perceives as a nearly endless expanse of unfinished basement stands a young woman before a curtain. An obscure glow, the source from somewhere

(*very cold and very dark*)

nearby. The curtain, reaching the ceiling, wraps around a cylindrical shape. A quote comes to mind for a reason beyond my immediate perception—"*when you stare into the abyss, the abyss stares back at you,*" by Nietzsche.

It makes me crave a cigarette. I've never smoked one before. Better late than never.

"When I called you 'Jake Sullivan,' I thought maybe you *were* your father," says Maggie.

"You knew him?"

She turns and looks at me like I'm stupid. Her face is a tenebrous wonder; it's all bending blacks and delicate angles.

"Obviously not his face." A pause. "But you look like how I *imagined* he would look, although when you came closer I saw you were my age. Then I remembered that"

(*which stares back*)

"your father had died . . ." She lets that linger, turns back toward the curtain, and then an almost supernatural nonchalance noticeably begins to override her posture, her mannerisms (fear finally roots itself at the base of my skull and tells me it's there and that I should be afraid—very, very afraid). She says, "Your mother called again."

I move a few fingers. My toes waggle. Tongue rims dry lips. I mumble out, "What's beyond the curtain?"

Ignoring me. "I told her I was your girlfriend and that she could leave a message. I don't think she believed me but she left a message. Said your *stepfather* called her. Spotted a woman in his apartment. She had a scar. He called her a . . . *mermaid.*" Maggie laughs.

"Samina?" My heart races. I need to see her.

Ignoring me again: "I should thank your father for everything I have here." She spins in a semicircle, arms open. "I went to a nice college; didn't have to spend a dime."

"What are you saying?"

Finally responding: "Baxter Daniel was not the man who killed my sister. While my mother was still in the hospital, your father and his partner—your ex-stepfather, the one who will be here shortly—showed her a few pictures. Asked if she recognized anyone. Her eyes grew wide when she saw Baxter Daniel's face. She pointed at him and said, 'He harassed me at the grocery store,' or maybe it wasn't a grocery store but you get the point.

"A few days later a lineup was presented before my mother. But this time she said Baxter was not the killer.

"'Why?' your father said.

"To which my mother said, 'Because he doesn't have long, pink nails; nor a tattoo on his left wrist.'

"'What kind of tattoo?'

"'It was odd,' she said, 'occult-looking'—"

I think about the occult symbol under my crib.

"—you sketched it on the photo you left in front of my apartment," I say, and now I'm able to sit up and lean against my elbow. The room is breathing in and out, expanding and contracting.

"You still don't understand, Jake. But you will." She goes up to the curtain and opens it just a slit so only she can peer inside. "He had my mother sketch out the symbol to the best of her ability and took it. A couple days later, he made a proposition, telling her that if on the witness stand she pointed out Baxter Daniel as *The Abortionist* then he would give her a monthly check of five hundred dollars until I turned eighteen. My mother loved me more than she hated the person who did this to her, not to mention the other women, so she reluctantly agreed. But she promised your father two things.

"One: that if he didn't bring the real *Abortionist* to justice, then she *would*—in her own way, in her own time.

"And two: that she would take away everyone responsible for my sister's death. Starting with the cops who looked the other way, then—"

"—me," I finish for her.

"Yes, his own children. Maybe the whole world."

My heart hammers in my chest, the freshly unburied memory of the playground swirling around my head. Spinning faster and faster.

"But your mother killed herself."

"It was the only way. You see, your father obviously—based on our current predicament—never followed through. I don't think he ever tried. Baxter Daniel was his man, and a monster in his own right. My mother's blood was necessary to fulfill her end of the bargain."

"But *The Abortionist* never killed again," I say. I want to tell her maybe her mother was wrong about the nails and tattoo. Instead I say, "I don't understand. What's all this about blood? Why'd you draw that symbol and leave that photo on the ground? Why'd your mother kill yourself in front of me?"

"She loved us so much that she was willing to die in order to bring my sister back to this temporal plane. And like all true forms of love—transcendent forms of love— it requires a sacrifice . . . of blood. My sister was shambling about the Night Place, and my mother turned on the light"

(*bleeding between the stars*)

"so my sister could find her way home—at least more frequently. I think she's almost here—"

Night Place! my mind shrieks at the mentioning of it.

But of course Maggie would have heard of it. If Samina is—or *was*—my best friend, she is likely much closer to her own sister.

That's when I hear underwater bubbles and a thrashing sound beyond the veil of curtains.

I struggle to give life to my feet and arms but they're drunkards snoozing off hangovers. A dull ache pulses up my body.

"Did you even look up what that symbol meant, Jake? I was trying to help you."

"Help me do what?"

"Help you *understand*."

I try to angle my right leg at a ninety-degree angle and push off to a one-legged standing position but I tumble forward and curse and in a hissy fit I yell out, "Understand *what?*"

"What this all means. That symbol on the back of the photo—the one my mother saw on the wrist of the person who killed my sister and left us for dead—it has a meaning. *Hyperfertility.* You know, there are apps in which you can snap a photo and the AI will instantaneously run it through millions of references and tell you to a near enough certainty what something is—whether it's a plant found near your house, a bug on the wall, a symbol. All thanks to a book called *The Passage of Oslo*, written by a survivor of a two-hundred-year-old death cult, that had been scanned and uploaded as PDFs to a website. This cult was fascinated with finding a Jacob's ladder into an array of earthly and *extra*earthly gifts. Everything from finding a lost sock to losing ten pounds, from becoming fertile for a healthy child to bringing back the sister of your only daughter.

"I only mention the app for your sake. As in *it's your fault for not digging a little deeper*. If you had, maybe you wouldn't have come here. At least your father didn't have that shortcut, but I think at the end of the day that your father didn't need one. Your father already knew what it meant. Already knew *who* it was. And *that's* really why he paid off my family—not to help us, not to get me through college. That's why he *chose* Baxter Daniel. A goat sent into the wilderness for the sins of a certain person close to him. Perhaps it worked, for a while. Ironically it only required the death of seven babies, as well as the intricate layout of the scenes of murder; of the mother below and the babe above; and the trickling, trickling, trickling of blood. From babe to mother. And the drinking of blood from both the mother and the child. If the media had known, they may have called the killer *The Vampire* instead, don't you think?"

"I don't think anything, lady," I say. Then I add, "If my dad had been giving your family money, my mother would have known."

She doesn't say anything.

"Why'd you give me that picture of Charlie? And the name *Herman Grusenmeye*r? That *was* you in front of my apartment, right? Had to have been." My calves and forearms had finally slept off their hangovers. My ass all the way up to my chest, however . . . still blackout drunk, an apocalyptic city

(*is a vat of acid*)

of bouncing back-and-forth nerves, the sizzling and throbbing sensation trying to climb up my ribcage and other adjacent bones.

"I prepared the picture, yes. I was trying to show you that you sent out into the wilderness your own goat. And—although unbeknownst to you (at least consciously)—for the very same reason that your father had."

"You're not making any fucking sense, woman!" My tongue feels like a half-dead slug, and I'm not certain how well I'm enunciating my words.

"Herman Grusenmeyer was a bad man, but not *your* man."

Defensive: "He had a history of violence, he hated cops and for good reason—his father was accidentally killed by one when he was a boy—and he *confessed*! He wrote a letter. He had a cop buried in his backyard, and half a head of a retired cop in his freezer. All *The Hot Tub Killer*'s victims were cops, and Herman sure as hell liked to kill cops."

"Then how did your partner Charlie get killed? Grusenmeyer had been in prison."

"Charlie had a heart attack swimming in the local pool."

"Did he seem like the type that would?"

"Would what?"

"Take a random swim during closed hours." She doesn't let me answer. "What about your father?"

"Accident—suicide—shit, I don't know—"

"The truth is, Jake, I think you knew who'd done it and wanted to choose your own societal sacrifice. Your father used Baxter, George W. Bush used Saddam, the Israelites used goats, and you used Herman. Listen, I'm not judging you. It's human nature. We all do it. And I appreciate it."

"Appreciate what?"

She laughs and looks at me, her head tilted like a dog.

"For protecting Samina, silly."

My throat constricts.

"We're fulfilling Mother's promises. She's sorry about Charlie, though. Charlie wasn't police during *The Abortionist*-killing spree, but he *did* see you and her talking on the day he was killed."

"I—"

"—don't remember, yes, you've made that point very clear. But she talks to you occasionally, and you know that *deep* in your bones. That's why it feels like trying to remember a dream after waking. That's why you suddenly get feelings of déjà vu; I get very similar *sensations* in her presence and the aftermath—except I see her more often and I think it *sticks* psychically or metaphysically or whatever you want to call it."

More bubbles. She peers between the curtains. When she speaks from across the expanse of primordial darkness of the basement, wherein the pitchy oblivion are a chasm of chaos and unseen serpents—dancing, fighting, *fucking*—it's echoey and infused with a drone of a low wind, *conchlike*, and all my meat vessel senses as I lay there weakly upon my elbow are bottlenecked to the eclipse of light where the young woman and the curtained-tank are.

"They'll be coming soon," she says, "and then it'll be only you and *The Abortionist* who remain. My mother's promises will be fulfilled. And you and her—the boy and girl at the crossroads, the babes of blood, Orphans of the Atercosm"

(*my heart pauses, then gallops*)

"will be united again.

"I see them now. He tried hiding in his bedroom. A closed door won't stop her, she'll find another door. *Make one.* He's on his bed now, she's walking up to him, his eyes are wide, her mouth is wider. He wants her, obviously. The old man's hand can't help itself, the sick fuck. Maybe one last grope before going to the Great Show Beyond. She's kissing him now—"

I can see in my mind's eye her mouth wrapping around his mouth, his face, his head, and her long, lush hair weaving in and out of his old man flesh.

"You love her," says Maggie, turning. "You're

jealous?"

And I don't know why I say what I say but I say it anyway. "Of course," I say.

"But she's your *sister*—half, anyway."

Now the throbbing and sizzling sensations of my ass and core have successfully climbed up my ribcage and other adjacent bones and I prop myself up at a better and more comfortable angle and I look at Maggie and I look at the turquoise sliver between the curtain. Do I see a leg floating in it? Then I remember what I'd just heard and I find purchase of the floor and push off and onto my wobbly feet and I say, "The fuck you just say?"

"Samina is your half-sister," Maggie repeats.

For the briefest of moments I imagine my dad going around Shepherdstown roughly nine months before I was conceived, in which he performed morbid acts of sexual contortionism to unwitting young women, and then to expunge the evidence he killed the woman and his offspring one by one by one—

—but that doesn't account for

(*hyperfertility*)

the tattoo and pink nails. Besides, Maggie had just told me that only *The Abortionist* and I remain.

Is my dad alive somehow, somewhere, somewhat, somewhen, somewhy?

I soon discover *yes* but *no*.

"THEY'RE COMING."

Maggie goes around the basement lighting previously unseen candles. Their flames are stagnant. They look like yellow-white teardrops raining down around us. The crying abyss reveals about the floor a series of chalk-drawn insignias. As if in answer to my bewildered observation:

"I want this to be perfect," she says. "For when the promises are fulfilled, she will be born into new flesh."

I'm not sure if she finally realizes that I'd been standing or if she'd known but didn't care to do anything till now, but she comes up to me and hugs me and kisses me on the mouth (I feel her tongue circle around my teeth and tongue), says something biologically unlikely considering her prior claims ("this is less weird since I'm not your sister; just imagine I have a scar"), and finds me an antique rocking chair to sit down on.

I do.

I have nothing else going on.

And to be honest, I *did* imagine Maggie having a scar when she'd kissed me; imagined us—me and not Maggie but Samina—in a tub in a candlelit room in a city that's full of opportunity and love, and we are sharing with each other our own opportunities and love. *Dimidium*-siblinghood be damned.

Then the curtained-tank begins to moan. Not like floorboards moaning when trod across but also not human. Not quite animal, either, but something else. Some impossible-to-place-a-finger-on OTHER.

Then, holding a candle in her own hand, its flame jittering only from her breath, she walks over to a table and grabs a sheet of printer paper and starts reading something in another language. It sounds like a mantra, a prayer. Aggressive and throaty; if cancer was a language, it would be this eldritch lingual abomination.

Did the candleflame grow? Is something growling from above? It did grow, that flicker in primordial darkness. The Shed Tear of the Leviathan in her hand and below her mouth is greedily sucking in and utilizing the discarded carbon dioxide as a building block, something between molten sorrow and wrathful gas; it dances to the rhythm of the cancerous incantation. Does something bark? Not a dog, but—

The Universe is aligned, it seems, at least temporarily, as the candleflames about the basement reveal their shared kinship—or a reverent sort of mimicry—to the Leviathan's Teardrop that dances below the fundamentally beautiful young woman's lips; between the curtains a turquoise glow bleeds out and penetrates into my eyes where it imbeds a nostalgia I can't articulate in this three-dimensional carcass; and the ceiling lights flicker only once, but I can see about the basement a slew of dry-aged and mummified abominations

(*a downpour of half-formed childhood memories come pounding against my skull, creating a flashflood of cerebral gunk and gangrenous phantasms and so much Goddamned pain; were these the kin of my hypnotically-suppressed pre-Samina "imaginary friends?" Were these the Orphans?*)

—that which the Abyss had aborted or that Samina had brought with her like a cat leaving gifts on a front porch doormat—shoved into its four corners. I also see this: at the top of the stairs stands a dim outline of a winged figure. More birdlike than Angelic. It's exercising deliberate stealth. Something in its hand. A finger to its mouth.

Shhh.

"The stars"—apparently at some point Maggie had begun speaking English (in the tank something is thrashing)—"o the stars."

She eats the Teardrop.

All at once the candles about the basement, and at the exact same moment, extinguish.

Perfect black, famished abyss, apotheotic beauty, consecrated void: it all comes washing over me, and I feel the hairs stand atop my neck and arms. An unscratchable itch in my brain. A lingering sort of melancholic angst as I wait for what's to come. The angst is pregnant with something I don't have the mental capacities to comprehend; or if I did, there would be no words; but I have neither the brain nor the words nor the eyesight to pierce the perfect abyss, the apotheotic void, that which looks upon me as a FATHER would a son.

More thrashing in the tank.

Something bangs against the side.

Again and again.

I think I'm still sitting down. Yeah, I am.

Maggie crosses the floor to the tank and reaches her hands to the curtains to draw them back (a *click!*) and when she does—and I see what I see in a filter of red after I hear what I hear—I realize that Maggie had been right. What is oozing down the now fully revealed tank is what transcendent forms of love require. Maggie had been right about something else, too: Samina and I are babes both born of blood.

A flash of lightning and its trailing clamorous roar.

I see all of this happen at once.

Now Maggie *does* have an imperfection. It's just below her eye. Whereas Samina only has a semicircular scar, as if from a bolt-gun, half of Maggie's face had been eaten by that which she had called forth, even if inadvertently: the other half of the promise: *The Abortionist.*

Another flash of lightning lingeringly endless.

I squint.

"*Jake?*"

Somehow it just now dawns on me that the reason why Maggie's face had disintegrated into a gory mess of gristle, bone, meat, and blood is because of the gun being held in a dainty, pink-nailed hand. My mother stands next to the light switch on the wood beam near the staircase. The half-formed aborted atrocities in the corners of the basement seem trivial compared to the three-ish occupants of the tank, two of them alive-ish. The other one—my brother Kyle—is water-bloated and stagnant, his eyes still open like gray, swollen grapes. Their black seeds looking at me. Accusing me. And perhaps the accusation isn't unjustified. Because it's my fault, isn't it, for sending out in the wilderness my Herman-goat instead of the culprit—Samina?

"Jake, let's go."

Mom reaches for me. When she does, the cuff of her (*wing*)

sleeve pulls toward her body. How many other times had I seen it as a boy and just hadn't thought of it? Lots of boys' mothers have tattoos. Sure they do. But this one matches the one on the back of Charlie's yearbook photo. She sees my eyes' trajectory. Embarrassed—*ashamed*—she pulls down the cuff.

"You were the only one I was meant to have," she says, as if this answered all my burning questions.

I confront her. "Why?"

"Because I *couldn't*, Jakey. Jake and I—Jacob, I mean—we . . . we tried and tried and tried and the doctors said I was barren. I was meant to be a mother, Jakey, I knew it. I was I was I was, but I couldn't. So I did what I could and I found a *True Religion*. A *book*—"

"*The Passage of Oslo*," I offer.

She's obviously not surprised I know this—considering the strange symbols chalked across the floor, the anatomical horrors crammed in the corners of the room, and the three swimmers in the vat of acid. My ex-stepfather's skin is dissolving; it's because of whatever substance is seeping through the gradually closing doorway above them where the third occupant, beautiful in a fundamentally flawed way, had come from; and in this process, my brother receives another dose of this corrosive agent and he's nothing but a gristly skeleton

105

with a hospital gown in mint-condition. The same is true with the old man. He's wearing what he'd worn when I went to see him. The extracosmic stuff only eats flesh.

"Yes," says Mom, pulling up her cuff and showing me the tattoo; "as is the Law of Conversion of Mass to matter, it is also to the creation of life, of the *soul*—and that's why I had to do what I did to those women and their unborn ones. I had to follow the ritual precisely. No corner-cutting, no half-assing. You wouldn't be here if I hadn't done what I'd done. You wouldn't be here without your Father's blessing."

"Dad would never—" I almost call Mom a "bitch" but hold my tongue. "That's why he killed himself, isn't it? This dark secret—protecting you out of . . . love, helping the Redmans out of guilt."

My mother is silenced. Her mouth twists in consternation, misery.

Something bangs on the tank.

It's Samina.

I wonder if she's suffocating. Am I supposed to let her out? Had her sister Maggie done this whole witchy shindig every time? Or was this a special moment? The *final* ritual? I stand up and my mother tries to pull me back. She might be telling me not to do it, that "she'll kill me, Jakey. She wants you all to herself, can't you see? She's always tried to take you away. Jacob never killed himself, son. One night he saw something in the bathtub with you. This was years after I found the symbol etched under your crib. I'd always thought it was Samina Redman, the mother, that she found me out, wanted revenge. Etched the symbol under your crib as . . ."

"*A promise*," I say.

". . . a threat," she counters. "When she killed herself, I thought it was all over. The police found her daughter Maggie in the car she'd taken, and I thought that *that* was who you were talking to when you were a boy. That maybe she was watching as her mother slit her own throat sitting next to you on the bench at the playground. That perhaps she came running out after Samina Redman did what she did. That that crying girl was seared into your mind. And that perhaps you manifested a coping mechanism in the form of Samina's living daughter, Maggie.

"But I was wrong."

Another bang on the glass.

The doorway to wherever she'd come from—some joint between the old man's apartment and this house, hundreds of miles away—is only a sliver now. I wonder why I'd never been affected by the acid when she'd come to visit me as a child. But in my bones I think I know.

The same reason she isn't.

Our siblinghood.

We're both Orphans of the Atercosm.

Mom: "At the time I thought it was just a gesture. That maybe it was Wiccan or some obscure pagan religion. A hex or whatever. But then, after Jacob swore to me that *something* was in the bathtub with you, I went in. *It* was gone. But etched—no, *burned*—into the tiled floor under the tub was the same symbol. I suppose the hypnosis worked so well that you never remembered *it* meeting with you. It disappeared—the symbol did—only thirty minutes later. I suppose, years earlier, if I hadn't put your crib on the side of the road, then it too would've vanished on its own. A *shame*; the crib was expensive."

My eyes wander to the ceiling above the tank. Sure enough, a symbol is etched—*burned*—into it. It looks like a rudimentary octopus or squid. Rotund; semicircular center; squiggly, angular lines branching out.

She sees it too, which seems to confirm her theories.

107

"It hadn't occurred to me until I found the symbol under the bathtub that it wasn't a threat, wasn't a pseudo-hex, wasn't even Samina Redman's doing it (remember, she was already dead, and you hadn't started talking to the girl until *after* the playground incident), but rather it was linked to what you used to call 'Orphans.'

"Shortly after, the dead girl with the scar killed your father; I know she did."

Mom turns away and begins walking toward one of the basement's corners, as if those horrors would act as a bulwark for the true horror of the words to come. Then the words come. She says. "Jacob and I had stopped trying altogether, Jakey. *The Abortionist* case had really affected his psyche—"

"—he didn't know that you were . . . ?" I ask.

She sighs. "Not until the bitch drew the fucking symbol at the hospital. Jacob thought I'd just . . . wanted a tattoo. I told him it had a secret meaning. That wasn't a lie, you know. And he thought nothing else of it." My mother laughs. She walks closer to the jammed-in-the-corner abominations. Kneels down and caresses the impression of mummified cranial orbit from a face as long as a horse's but oddly humanoid in its death-frozen expression twisted in agony. It somehow looks familiar, like a forgotten friend, like a half-sibling.

"*We're all Orphans of the Atercosm,*" I whisper so low that only their lingering psychic presences can hear. They can. Because, as Mom implied, *souls can't be created or destroyed, only transferred—altered—reassembled—always there—haunting.* Then Mom says:

"You were conceived on the night I botched the final ritual. But Jacob never came home that night. He'd been working the case—and"—she emphasizes slowly—"*yet. You. Were. Conceived.*"

Maggie had already implied as much, but it still takes me a moment to digest everything.

"That doesn't make sense. Everyone says I look like—"

"And you do, Jakey; I think your *True Father* wanted you to fit in, so you wouldn't look like one of these . . . *motherless things.*"

Now she stands from her knee. Her finger—in her upward motion—drags too harshly against the *motherless thing* with the horseface and the too-long teeth and the twisted posture. It moves mechanically. Joints deranged after years of deathly stagnancy. I hear its stale bones *clicking* as it hunkers even more flatly to the floor, where in the trickery of ceiling lights gives the illusion in the sockets of its eyes of remaining life. My mom must think this, too. She hops away quickly and then she breathes out deeply, realizing she'd made it move.

And while she is briefly distracted by this, I make my way to the tank. I step over Maggie. A stepladder leans against the side on the right, half-concealed by the bunched-up curtains. On my tippytoes I see a hatch on top. A padlock keeps it locked. Samina's face is close to mine; in my periphery is a phantasmagorical smear of inhuman and eldritch beauty, her blurred outline humming inside my brainpan; and I feel her eyes poring over me, or maybe even—on a psychic plane—*pouring* with a letter "u," lathering me—no, *marinating* me—with her arcane love.

(And I can only tell you that the reason I didn't look at her, at least not directly, was because I believed that if I did—if my eyes slid down and drank in her unfiltered beauty—then I would've sat there for days at the ALTAR OF VOID, admiring her form until I starved to death.)

I turn and kneel and dig my fingers into the pockets of the dead woman's legs, but her blood makes my hands stick to the fabric. It's hard to reach my fingers in all the way. Mom asks what I'm doing, but, ignoring her, I only do what I'm doing as I flip over the fresh corpse. I, as *unnecrophiliacally* as possible, grope Maggie's ass. The smell hits me after my fingers brush against the soft, warm lump. But next to what evacuated from her bowels is something small and metallic. I dig my fingers into her left butt pocket. It smells worse than death. I gag. I purchase the key in my hand and gag again and take the

(*what are you doing, Jakey*
don't let it out, Jakey
don't don't don't Jakey
Jakey Jakey Jakey)

stepladder from the side and I half-think as I unfold it and step onto the first rung, then the second, that my mother will shoot me dead.

But she doesn't.

I insert the key and twist. The padlock snaps open and I fling it over my head. It clangs to the cement floor and slides and hits with a low thud into what I believe to be one of the *motherless things*. Then I open the hatch.

The water radiates with cold.

I think the bang I hear is a gun going off and the thump I hear a body hitting the floor. The final promise is fulfilled: *The Abortionist* is ended.

I look down in there and see three indistinct figures. It's clear that the one moving—the one rising—is Samina. My half-sister, my love. I was conceived when she bled onto her mother. I, a soon to be witness of her pale glory with undeserving eyes, await her ascension. Bloody bubbles grow huge and pop at the vat's foamy top. Its acid sizzles against my skin but doesn't burn. And bleeding between—bleeding *through*—the Atercosm and into my reality, the crown of her head breaks the water's surface; and that which I've sought my entire life, as it rises higher and higher, finally stares back into my eyes; and it says to me, "I want to take you somewhere very cold and very dark"; and then I'm pulled in, pulled forever, as the perfect black prays for stars and suns, and the famished abyss hungers for slop and chum, and the apotheotic beauty, which has that scar I love, is and always has been the consecrated void. The scar is a cracked-open doorway brimming with acid. I open it all the way and crawl through.

A FORLORN THING. An impassive watcher. A formless creature drenched in lonesomeness, despite the forever-company of its contorted children; of indifference, despite the sobbing of their suffering and pleading for mercy, for light. I watch in discombobulated terror as its great appendage swings back and forth like a blind idiot. Other Orphans dart deep into the surrounding grottos. Samina tries to get me to my feet. She does and I stumble and look down and see the naked corpse of a human woman, half-dissolved from her trip through the tunnel. I look at Samina. Then the appendage of the Forlorn Thing finds her and wraps its oily tendrils around her and pulls her up to what must be a head, for it has one great yellow eye like a lightless sun and something else that might be a mouth. It suddenly kisses her. Its lips wrap around her, engulfing her entirely. She is annihilated under a veil of black-rotted flesh. Lips, I think. A rumbling. It's chewing. When she is finally spit out and plops to the ground by my feet, she is a bloodless husk, arms warped at unnatural angles. I look up at the head of the Great Thing whose lips leak torrents of red-black blood. She's dead again, dead forever. But I am happy that my True Father doesn't see me. It never knew I existed.

Then I close my eyes, count to three . . .

". . . AND I WOKE UP IN this strange lobby, at this lonely motel"—he vaguely knew, but didn't know *how* he knew, it was called LUNARIS DEVERSORIUM, and had no idea how to pronounce it—"on this desolate highway, sitting next to you, with that monster movie playing on the TV over there."

He couldn't help but stare at the TV over the hunched bulk of the red-haired sleeping clerk, tucked in the office's corner like a dark secret; couldn't help but be entranced by the primordial shark lying on the beach of too-white sand, a terrible bird—the grandfather of all eagles—perched atop, and a midnight-black ooze seeping out the fishy carcass where great talons impaled it. It looked familiar, that ooze. Looked like a finger.

"That's quite a story, all right," said the woman, causing the man's head to snap toward her. He saw her—maybe for the first time, or maybe he'd known her from before, or maybe . . .

"I know you from somewhere, don't I? I swear I've seen you," said the man, snapping his fingers. "Valerie or Valentine . . . ?"

"Valora," she said. "Valora Williams."

ARTIFACT

"It is a fearful thing to fall into the hands of the living God."

—Hebrews 10:31

". . . for I knew that the King in Yellow had opened his tattered mantle and there was only God to cry to now."

—Robert W. Chambers

THE HAND

I

THE WITCHING HOUR IS UPON me . . . and I've just enough pencil to write this. I see through the window, through the demonic nebulous hovering over the sea, the shape of its seven Fingers—seven because that's the number of Yahweh—connected to its colossal unshapen Palm. Seven, not because it is God, but because it wishes to be. An envious Shape full of malice, of hunger.

Do I have thirty minutes?

Less?

It shouldn't take long to tell you this. To tell you what to do with the BOOK on the desk. Don't look too closely at its form. You mustn't let the symbol unravel behind your eyelids, for it contains an **u**ndeserved knowledge.

Some gods want acknowledgement, like Yahweh; other gods—such as the one whose Hand is floating over sea and soon beach and village, then finally, to still the storm inside my psychosphere, the space I've made into a study at the top of this stone lighthouse—want desolate aloneness . . .

. . . so they can dream. And they stir when their names are uttered, so beware whose name you even whisper-think. It may be an irate one.

I cannot describe to you its form because it is

unstructured in our small human minds; and its name I cannot tell you because if I do . . . its shape you shall see and know intimately and yet—despite knowing it in all its awesomeness, every detail, every dead universe buried in its membranous casing—you don't have the mental machinery to process the concepts into language in which to tell another living soul. Even if possible (I've wasted enough time as it is to explain to you that it isn't), it will reach out its deific Hand and embrace you before the words can be spilled onto page. You can't hide from it. You've summoned it from its slumber, even if inadvertently, and it—made of inorganic flesh; a soulless presence; a wretched, undead shadow—will snuff you out completely.

NOISE DOWNSTAIRS—

Is it the pattering of rain moving in strange patterns? Or the erratic footfalls of a large group of people standing uncomfortably close to one another, all wearing tap dancing shoes, just tapping and tapping and tapping?

Yes, let's say a group of Kachuwaians clustered together (all wearing tap dancing shoes, ha ha) are coming to check up on the American visiting their village for the sake of enlightenment, the one becoming progressively (and I may say *aggressively*) more and more erratic for each image his brain absorbs from the BOOK. Or are they not? Is the man who shares the same face as I not even in Kachuwa any longer? Are the images from the emblem on the BOOK transferring him elsewhere—perhaps even *downloading* him from Sol's third planet in the twenty-first century to some blasted void where time and space have no conclusive meaning? And if the footfalls are not of an illogically clustered group of Kachuwaians or strange patterns of rainfall, what would he—which is to say *I*—see if his/my eyes glide across the quasi-atemporal form of that which is making those wretched *tapping* sounds? Would it be some grotesque anatomical creature shaped in the image of its Creator? Is it the Eyes and Ears of the Hand? Or is it the Mouth?

I'VE COME BACK FROM INVESTIGATING the nois**e** (there are two bookcases in front of the door now; I don't exactly remember doing it, but I certainly know *why* I did). Found nothing in the lower depths of the light-house. So I ventured into the village. Regarding its physical layout, it remained seemingly untouched. But the Kachuwaians were gone. Sheltering themselves from the sea storm, most likely. However, I could not discover the source of the abysmal *tap dancers*. Raindrops, I hypothesized. Yes, heavy raindrops, and the stone corridors had amplified the noise, crafting in my fragile, susceptible mind illogical imaginings.

Yes.

A stress-induced psychotic break *should be* the most plausible explanation. You may be thinking (as was I very briefly) that upon gazing into the seaward sky, I had misidentified those dark storm clouds as a giant Hand in the same way one may see white fluffy clouds shaped like bunnies. Perhaps the phantasmagorical TE**X**T expanding across my mind from the BOOK (which is very much a painstakingly detailed ritual manual, one practiced

—*it stares at me from across my study could the* BOOK *be Its mouth and the*

oh god god GOD
oh Jesus Christ

117

process yes the process is different from energy produc-
tion as we understand it perhaps first it eats then it Sees
and Hears and finally grabs with its Hand—

with religious fervor in a nearly forgotten era) only put me on edge.

I've spent the better part of five years doing research on folklores and anecdotes on what, in Hebrew—and from a different text (one written by a French philosopher many hundreds of years ago) excavated on the outskirts of Ashdod, Israel—loosely translates to *The Book of the Hand of the Five Anteriors*: which is to say, the relic which lay on this desk. I've ruined relationships, burned bridges, and established drug addictions all for my love of ancient, obscure pagan religions. But this one in particular takes the cake. I'd been obsessed with this nameless Hebrew text. Spent five hours a day researching it. Traveled to referenced cities from that tome—searching, investigating, praying. And finally I found the cookie crumb trail that led me to the oddly preserved Kachuwa village on the far outskirts of Russia. I finally found it, the actual BOOK. So perhaps you may furthermore be thinking that when I had found *The Book of the Hand of the Five Anteriors,* it had literally overloaded my brain and that the Hand was only a psychotic fabrication of said adult-onset psychosis and that it wasn't there—never was—never could be—*how* could it?—only clouds, yes—*dark dark dark*—clouds, absolutely—shaped like a seven-fingered Hand . . .

(That was what I had hoped for, too: "temporary insanity.")

. . . and down there, where the lighthouse leaked into the ancient but well-preserved Kachuwa village, when I tilted my weary, sleep-deprived head to the seaward sky, I saw those dark clouds. For a moment, at least, that's all there was. And relief washed over me tremendously. Then a noise—

Dashing across the rain-wet cobblestone street had been a man clutching tightly in his arms, which flapped wildly in the violent wind, a wool blanket. Then he was gone, into his home where a scared wife and a lachrymose boy awaited him. As I had sanguinely hoped for: I was not (at least not literally) downloaded to another era. Instead—and I had assumed as much—the villagers had taken shelter against the oncoming storm. The man with the blanket reassured me of this.

Then I looked up again quite by accident (if I hadn't, I wouldn't be writing you this right now). One Finger, and then another, then five more, all seven extending themselves from the ever-closer sea-hovering thunderhead. The Hand had reformed itself.

I NOW REALIZE THAT THE Kachuwaians see the storm in the same way stick figures on a flat sheet of paper can see only the dot on the paper, not the pen making the dot, let alone the hand holding the pen. *The Book of the Hand of the Five Anteriors*, after looking at it for so long, had flipped over my eyes a pair of 4D glasses. *I* can see the Hand, but the villagers cannot. And yet, sadly, they will not be peacefully swept into oblivion—for the storm is terrible in its own right, and mortal fear had been etched into the face of the blanket-clenching man and his wife and son whose fists twisted and turned over his bloodshot crying eyes, twisted and turned regarding the tremendously twisting and violently turning sea and the firmament creeping like black mold from unknowable celestial chasms which hover over the sea and the land, and the wind strong enough to hurl across the streets an apocalyptic ballad of left-out furniture and children's toys; flailing, suffocating fish and flapping, broken birds;

119

and shards of broken glass and tumbling driftwood and parts of boats and buckets . . .

. . . and yet perhaps it is a mercy to fear, even fatally, the materialistically perceived ink-leaking pen and not that which holds it—for there are things of and around this earth, above and below the heavens, and within and without space and time which are much worse than death; let alone the fear of it.

HOW LONG HAD I STARED at the sky, unmoving? It was finally the disorderly and bombastic clicking and clacking of the *tap dancers* that broke my paralysis.

Turning slowly but not all the way I saw, peripherally, a ghastly, impossible contour. Then my feet ran. They took me back to the lighthouse, back to the makeshift study, then my hands moved the bookshelves in front of the door and picked up this dwindling pencil to finish my warning.

So perhaps I am having a psychotic break, of sorts . . . but that doesn't make what is happening any less real.

I DON'T THINK THE *TAP dancers* know how to open doors, but they—the Eyes, the Ears, *whatever*—know where I'm a**t**. That's enough. And the Hand won't need to open the door; for its enormity can fit the entire village into its Palm and sweep it out of existence.

The ground is vibrating.

Everything is static.

Sun is blotted out.

My name is Walter Elliot-Washington Grayson. I'm a professor at **[dark stain]** Please send this letter to my friend K **[dark stain]** enson, a professor at **[dark**

stain] Illinois, and tell him to smash this God-damned **[dark stain]** if there's any trace of it. Tell him that **[dark stain]** *of the Hand of the Five Anteriors*, and **[dark stain]**.

THE SHAPE IS OVER ME.

II

HEY BILL,

Just received shipment from Russ. embassy. Crate consisting of

(a) *COMPLETE SKELETON* (no clothing articles);

(b) *WALLET W/ AMERICAN* PASSPORT (name illegible);

(c) *LETTER W/ DARK STAINS*;

(d) *STONE W/ INSIGNIA ETCHED INTO SURFACE.*

All found on Sea of Okhotsk shore. Plz process ASAP, when the materials arrive @ ur lab.

Prolly hoax, but there's Mr Skelly w/ an American passport...... so, u know, better safe than sorry?

- D

III

DEAR PROFESSOR JORGENSON,

I've been unable to reach you via phone, so please forgive the impersonal approach which is this email. However, it may be all the better to electronically relay this information. A phone call may not do it justice. Also, email allows me to send you a copy of the letter of interest, which I will discuss shortly.

Firstly, my name is William Tulsi. I'm a lab specialist and consultant for the CIA. I'm contacting you because I have in my possession a letter written by, allegedly, a Dr. Walter Elliot-Washington Grayson. And it *seems* to have been addressed to you. I say "seems" because most of this information is unreadable via dark stain, as you will notice upon opening the attached file. The stain is blood. I could make out "K" as in **K**arl; "enson" as in Jorg**enson**; and "Illinois," as in Sharp Point, **Illinois**, so I took a chance. It's *there* where you live, if my sources are up to date. Plus, considering the subjects you teach at the university, it seems logical you are the right recipient.

Initially, due to its preposterousness, not to mention frustrating vagueness, I didn't take the letter seriously upon its arrival at my lab. It was found near the Sea of Okhotsk, Russia, next to the skeletal remains of a human male, a wallet, and a strange stone object. Any evidence of identification had been in a state of *progressive decay*; the nationality on the passport was however legible, thus the embassy's involvement followed swiftly by the CIA's. I believe this to be a hoax, to be certain— for instance, if a man thought his death was quickly imminent, he would not have inserted a hidden code in the text. Seems to have been premeditated. You may have noticed throughout the letter that he had under-

122

lined a series of characters, not to mention retracing the letters to bolden them.

Each character, chronologically ordered, spells out four words:

I used to exist.

Ironically, nowhere in the world does a Walter Elliot-Washington Grayson exist. Of course there are Walter Graysons, but not as many as one might assume, and they *all* have alibis, and none of them have "Elliot-Washington" as a middle name. Also, it's important to note that there is no record of there ever being a Kachuwa village or a Kachuwaian people, not in Russia nor anywhere else in the world nor at any point in history. It doesn't even sound *very Russian*, to be frank.

It would be easy to chalk this letter up as someone's imaginative and intricate attempt at fiction. Especially considering the age of the skeleton is at least a hundred years old. Except the results for the stain on the letter had come back positive for blood. So I have to take it *moderately* seriously for that reason alone—even though it's obvious the skeletal remains is not the blood's owner, and there isn't enough blood for any immediate red flags. Probably dug out of a grave and staged.

But I'm reaching out to you all the same. Just in case I'm missing something. Perhaps the name "Walter Elliot-Washington Grayson," along with the name of the village, isn't the man's *actual* name, nor the village's title, but a code for something that you'd only understand.

Walter Elliot-Washington Grayson is not a real person; but you are.

I hope this email reaches you in a timely fashion. I'll try calling again in a few days if I don't receive a response. I'd like to close this case as soon as possible because this is giving me the heebie-jeebies. I swear I'm even hearing these so-called "*tap dancers.*"

Thank you for your time,
Will

IV

DEAR MR. TULSI,

What you have sent me is perplexing to say the least. I do believe, based on the legible words at the end of the letter, and the fact that I know what "book" the writer speaks of, that this was indeed meant for me. However, I do not know a Walter Grayson (and if, as you say, it is meant as *code*, then I'm equally in the dark as for its meaning), let alone a Kachuwa village.

The Book of the Hand of the Five Anteriors is a fabled artifact. Although I believe it may still exist—and *used to*, for an absolute fact—it has never resurfaced in the modern world. It is peculiar that our John Doe knows its title: only a handful of living scholars know its name and none of us know its literal contents.

However, the forementioned untitled Hebrew text—the one excavated from the outskirts of Ashdod—is real; and unless one specializes in my particular field and has certain ins with elite academia circles (for a lack of a better term), then this text should not have been known about. Not just by anyone, if you can forgive my snobbery. I can count on one hand how many people have seen the old tome, and half of one hand how many people have *successfully* translated and analyzed it—and I'm one of them.

Maybe one of my colleagues' computers—Hell, maybe even mine—had been hacked, and this is, as you believe, a prank; one in which the prankster went above and beyond. For what reason, I cannot fathom.

But, as you also pointed out, I don't think there's enough blood to be concerned. I'd say it would be relatively safe to close this case.

If there's anything else I can help you with, I'll be happy to help.

Sincerely,
Karl Jorgenson

V

DEAR PROFESSOR JORGENSON,

Out of curiosity, based on the "untitled" Hebrew text, does what this alleged Walter Grayson had said about the Hand and the *tap dancers* make any sense at all? The answer probably means nothing, but I want to be thorough nonetheless.

I suppose, Professor Jorgenson, what is eating at me is this: why *such* an elaborate "prank" for an obscure historical document? The Russians could have easily chosen to dismiss this entirely—even with the skeleton, even with the blood, which is way too old for the murderer, *IF* there is a murderer, to be alive, *IF* that was the intention of theoretical prankster; or for the cause of death to have any kind of significance whatsoever due to the passage of time.

Do you see the paradox here?

If this person is intelligent enough to hack a computer for information on such a book, and to effectively use some kind of chemical to radically deteriorate the wallet and all its contents—not to mention having a significant amount of creativeness to incorporate all the obscure details into the letter, stuff only you and a few others would know about—then the prankster should have been smart enough to know that the skeletal remains were too old, and the blood too conservative an amount.

And let's not forget the sophisticated complexity of this prank in a broader sense: the computer hacking, the grave robbery, the carefully constructed writing, and staging all of this on a Russian beach. (I suppose it could be a Russian civilian prank, but still.)

It doesn't add up.

Maybe it's not supposed to?

Anyway, as I mentioned, if I could know more on the hypothetical/religious/historical aspects of the Hand, the Book, the *tap dancers*, and the Five Anteriors, that might help me make sense of this otherwise senseless case.

Also, you seemed more disturbed that a Random Nobody had access to this niche research than by the content of the letter itself. Which makes me wonder that maybe, to you, the letter *did* make sense.

Will

VI

MR. TULSI,

The Book of the Hand of the Five Anteriors, in theory, and referenced only three times in the untitled Hebrew text, is a catalyst to allow a sort of "Jacob's ladder"; i.e., an ascent into "Heaven." Although it should be said that this "Heaven" isn't the Judeo-Christian version: it's something else, and I'm only using "Heaven" as a substitution. (In the early 1700s a woman called Helga the All-Witch had claimed to have "read" the Book and had written a chapter of it—one you can find online, in fact—called *The Passage of Oslo,* should you be interested in such an intellectual detour.)

I suppose I'll have to unpackage your questions carefully, but also streamline it heavily, as to avoid my writing a five-thousand-word essay.

Firstly, as for the *tap dancers*, that's a head-scratcher; but it would make sense that they are, as the writer suggested, the Eyes and Ears of the Hand (which I'll discuss in a moment). You could call them agents or emissaries. The equivalent, perhaps, to Angels if we use Christianity as a point of reference.

The Five Anteriors is a term used (and certainly not word for word) in ancient, mostly forgotten cults for five beings, or "gods," that predate all organized religions—hence the word "anterior," which literally means "coming before in time." They come from *outside* our known universe and our space-time continuum; therefore sometimes they're referred to as the Outer Ones. Nothing is known of their individual names or forms—except for one, an entity referred to as Draguana (sometimes called the Bright One, the Serpent from Beyond, or Ol' Lucy of the Starlight), which, detailed in the Hebrew tome, had some craftsmanship in the creation of the Hand.

Finally, the Hand …

Whether or not it is canonical with Anterior lore is a rather messy affair—at least academically speaking. Similar to Judeo-Christianity's Apocryphal writings, the author's authenticity is in question.

Plainly speaking, Jean Castiel DuFort, the French philosopher who [allegedly] wrote the Hebrew text which our John Doe discussed briefly—not so different from our John Doe himself—never existed. That's another reason so few in my field have actually studied the text—same reason, I imagine, Jewish or Christian scholars don't regularly study the Apocryphal books.

But here lies the debate.

The very nature of the Hand *could* explain the author's metaliteral nonexistence. Some believe (even ones who reject the Hebrew text's legitimacy) that the Hand represents the Shadow of Draguana. As mentioned, this Anterior had at least some role in the Hand's creation, so it might make sense for the Hand's characteristics to relate to that which created it: in this case, meaningful contrast: an inversion (whereas others believe Draguana and the Hand are synonymous, and this train of thought goes so far as to say that the Serpent in the garden of Eden, the one that tempted Eve, wasn't an actual serpent—but one of the fingers of the Hand, which is to say Draguana, hence its sometimes being referred to as the Serpent from Beyond).

This is what DuFort wrote—at least, this is the best English translation; but still doesn't capture the essence of the original Hebrew text:

> *Draguana is a Weaver;*
> *the Hand is an Expunger.*

Draguana draws; the Hand erases.

DuFort theorized *The Book of the Hand of the Five Anteriors*—as the story goes—always gets lost in time because those who find it are simply ... snuffed out of existence. Not just killed, but totally wiped out. First he—DuFort—went totally mad and forgot himself, and then, echoing this, the world went mad and forgot him, too.

DuFort believed, as well, that *that* was happening to him at the time of his writing of the nameless text; that reality was dissolving around him, blurring his definitions. So perhaps the only thing that remained of him was the Hebrew text. Maybe the Hand—theoretically speaking, of course—can't manipulate or "expunge" written words, but only *Homo sapiens* him- or herself, and the collective memory of said human.

Also, this:

Although DuFort never put a code into his work like Grayson did, he did state something of comparable meaning. This was the second to last line of the Hebrew text:

I once existed.

I hope my explanations help you understand the broader picture of Anterior lore.

Karl Jorgenson

VII

DISPATCHER: *911, what's your emergency?*

JOHN DOE: [heavy breathing]

DISPATCHER: *911, what is your—*

JOHN DOE: *They're outside.*

DISPATCHER: *Is your address 294 Redmont Ave, Grand-ville, Massachusetts?*

JOHN DOE: *Yes. They're outside my house.*

DISPATCHER: *Who is, sir? What is your emergency?*

JOHN DOE: *I . . .* [indecipherable whispering]

DISPATCHER: *Are they armed?*

JOHN DOE: *Aluminum.*

DISPATCHER: *Sir, can you clarify?*

JOHN DOE: [heavy breathing, hissing]

DISPATCHER: *Sir, I need—*

JOHN DOE: *Baseball bats, I think; yes, aluminum baseball bats.*

DISPATCHER: *Are they threatening you, sir?*

JOHN DOE: *OF COURSE THEY ARE, GODDAMNED MOTHERFUCKER!* [starts crying]

DISPATCHER: [sighs] *Sir, I understand your stress. What are they doing with the baseball bats?*

JOHN DOE: *They're clanking the sides of my house. So . . . so many bats, CAN'T YOU HEAR THEM?*

DISPATCHER: *Can you tell me how many there are?*

JOHN DOE: *Many.*

DISPATCHER: *Can they get in the way you got in?*

JOHN DOE: [panting] *I've got the only key.*

DISPATCHER: *Sir, can you give me the address? And your name?*

JOHN DOE: *294 Redmont Ave in Grandville: I confirmed that already. Send the cops—for God's sake, send the fucking cops.*

DISPATCHER: *And, sir, can you repeat your name?*

JOHN DOE: *William Tulsi. I live here. Oh God, make them stop! That noise!*

DISPATCHER: *I can't hear anything, sir; listen—*

JOHN DOE: *That's because they're* tapping . . . *ever so* lightly. *Just* tapping. [laughs] Tap. Tap. Tap. *Like* . . . *like* . . . [muffled]

DISPATCHER: *Sir, listen—you're going to have to be honest with me, or I'm going to chalk this up as a prank. Wait . . .* [sigh] *Sir, have you taken anything?*

JOHN DOE: *Anything? What?*

DISPATCHER: *Sir, have you taken any drugs? Anything hallucinogenic? LSD, DMT—anything of that nature?*

JOHN DOE: *I don't do drugs; I don't even drink.*

DISPATCHER: [impatient] *Then you're giving me the*

wrong address, sir, or you're lying about your ownership of the residence, because there is no William Tulsi who lives at 294 Redmont Ave in Grandville, Massachusetts. That particular house is foreclosed. You cannot have the key, sir. Also, if there were a group of people with baseballs bats trying to break into the house, we would have gotten calls from neighbors—regardless of it being three in the morning.

JOHN DOE: [crying]

DISPATCHER: However, *this is what I'm going to do: I'm sending a unit over to the address. They'll bring you to the hospital. They'll detox whatever it is you've taken. Please stay where you're at. And sir . . . don't run.*

JOHN DOE: [muffled]

DISPATCHER: *Sir, can you repeat?*

JOHN DOE: [heavy breathing] *They won't find me. I was never here.* [gasp] *Oh God, oh—in the sky. It's coming for me, to scoop me up, snuff me out, rapture me like . . . like Enoch and Elijah. It's coming, it's coming.*

[faint tapping sounds]

DISPATCHER: *What's coming?*

JOHN DOE: *The Hand.*

NOCTURNIUM

"So then because thou art lukewarm, and neither cold nor hot, I will spue thee out of my mouth."

—Revelation 3:16

FOREWORD

I feel as though *Nocturnium* warrants a little extra clarification as to what you, Dear Reader, are about to get yourself into. It's not a short story; rather, it's the prologue and first chapter of what I consider my magnum opus. While my earlier work, *Native Fear*, bore the hallmarks of literary horror in its prose and structure, infused with heavy and very dark A24esque themes involving race, rape, and religion (alas, all the taboo r-words—*oopsie*), it also served as a heartfelt homage to the *Resident Evil* videogame franchise. In essence, I wrote the novel that I'd want to read. Hindsight reveals why my venture failed to fully infiltrate the intended audience—too weighty for the *Resident Evil* crowd, too genre-centric—perhaps *niche*—for the serious fiction reader.

Nocturnium, however, takes a distinct narrative trajectory, embracing the realm of pure literary horror. It materialized in my creative sphere nearly a decade subsequent to *Native Fear*. If my debut novel occasionally exhibited echoes of Stephen King intertwined with a dash of Cormac McCarthy (by all means, we are what we read), then *Nocturnium* marks the point where my prose has attained a certain, shall we say, *equilibrium*. The passage of time and the recent-ish influence of authors such as Thomas Ligotti and Algernon Blackwood—as well as contemporary horror writers like Adam Nevill, Philip Fracassi, Josh Malerman, and Nick Cutter—have collectively acted as a kind of "activated charcoal," extracting the excesses of King's sway (e.g., protracted paragraphs, long sentences [and single sentences that are multiple paragraphs long (no, you didn't misread that)], parentheses within parentheses and sometimes within more parentheses, intricate subplots, etc.). In *Nocturnium*, you'll still find some of that stylistic flair, but it's more disciplined and calculated; and it's a lot less "imitative" of King, McCarthy, and Lovecraft. *Nocturnium* is what I hope a literarily matured C. F. Page reads like.

As mentioned earlier, *Nocturnium* stands as the *pièce de resistance* of my current bibliography. However, despite its weighty significance in my personal and creative life, I've chosen to steer clear of self-publishing; and thus, consequently, the possibility of *Nocturnium*'s release remains uncertain. If you're inclined to do so, skipping this excerpt and waiting for the finalized creation is perfectly reasonable. It's worth noting, though, that a caveat exists: the finished product may never see the light of day if the traditional publishing avenue remains elusive.

Without further ado, I present to you a glimpse of my very personal novel:

Nocturnium.

FIRST PROLOGUE

—THE SHAPE OF THE CALL—

I

I'M AFRAID OF ERIC EEL

weren't quite the last words uttered from Elisa Thoss-macher's mouth as she—with a disease-withered hand, nails brittle, lesions oozing with pus and blood, and knotted veins like mutated worms under her once (and not too long ago) youthful skin—shakily reached over to her steadfast husband sitting by her side. An envelope shook turbulently between alabastrine fingers.

Manikin fingers.

Tears brimmed behind his puffed eyelids.

"Who's Eric?" he said by way of humoring her. Maybe humoring himself. Ever since her mind had begun slipping into the abstract—*had* been for weeks, in fact—he knew that this *Eric Eel* must have been arbitrary; however, he'd never have guessed she was only nine words away from annihilation absolute.

Give to Kyle

she said, letting go of the envelope and the letter it contained.

He took the envelope. Mindlessly sliding it into the inside pocket of his navy cardigan, he said softly—a whisper that tiptoed on the edge of her fading consciousness as not to exacerbate her pain, and almost apologetically—"We don't know where he's at, Elisa."

He tried holding the hand she'd delivered the envelope in, but she was deceptively strong or plainly stubborn and pulled away, and raising her quivering finger she pointed somewhere over his shoulder. He saw only wallpaper, the partially shuttered window, a genesis of spiderweb, and three lit candles ("the ceiling light," she'd told him repeatedly, with a dejected insistence, "burns holes in my brain") flickering on the desk.

Opaque rheum ran down from her eyes and nose. Tinted in the liquescent downward slithering snake were rose-pink, specks of black, and tears. And then her final words:

They're going to eat him, Wallace.

Esoteric.

Random.

A secularist would say "a misfiring of neurons in the brain."

But still . . . the words hung there. In the air. Almost palpable. With shape and color and an echo. Pregnant with an ominous truth or un-truth that left him chilled to the bone.

"Hon?"

The last rays of pre-autumn sun cut through the shutter slats and made a strange crosshatch of lifeless light on her face, distorting her features. Already a charnel gray had begun crawling into her face from some bodily alcove labeled DEATH, and pressed outward, pushing away the color.

And *still* she pointed somewhere behind his back, her necrosed hand—*darkening darkening darkening*—wobbling: a tree branch in a light breeze.

During a long exhale her hand dropped suddenly, slamming into his large, callused palm. The suddenness startled him. Jerked his arm. Elbowed a small stack of books on her nightstand. They shifted over. Bumped into a lit pumpkin spice candle. The hot wax column jiggled briefly before becoming as moveless as Elisa.

"Elisa.

"Elisa?

"*Elisa!*"

No inhale.

Elisa had retreated into the labyrinthine corridors of her deteriorated, vacant mind: an empty vessel.

Bending over, he pressed his lips to her cold ones. (Wallace didn't know it presently, but she'd very soon be cremated.) Blistering tears welled behind his eyelids. Heavy. Hot. Acidic. And he looked once more over his shoulder and realized what she'd been pointing at.

Had the A/C not kicked on, he would not have noticed what lay on the desk flapping like a dying albino bat. But now that he saw it, he couldn't unsee it—not with the way it moved creaturelike, not with the way it glowed in the

(*moony dreamlight*)

moribund candlelight.

Sprawled out like a flayed creature lay, crinkled and overread, the long and multi-paged letter from her son Kyle. It in fact was the only letter from Kyle since THE ARGUMENT and his vanishing. Kyle—cunning and stubborn like his mother—had severed all ties, changed his phone number, and erased his digital presence. Elisa had fervently sought him through their neighbor's social media accounts, but her efforts yielded no results. Perhaps Kyle had anticipated her desperation and blocked not only Mindy Redman's accounts but also those of *all* their neighbors and relatives; that, or he *actually* did what few in the modern world could do: untether himself from the machine completely. The boy possessed a meticulousness that belied his years. The quivering letter, delivered a year prior, had remained a mystery to Wallace. Elisa guarded its contents jealously, never divulging its secrets. And Wallace, respecting her privacy, had refrained from prying or snooping.

The envelope Kyle had sent the letter in peaked its corner from under the letter itself. Wallace, not yet crying (part of him—despite the vamped-up *livor mortis* not only already discoloring her flesh but almost . . . *disfiguring it*, like some awful death-metamorphosis—thought she was resting, with the way she lay in somnolent stillness), stood waveringly. The floor beneath his feet swayed. Wriggling tiers of *moony dreamlight* swam like eels about the colorless room between he and the letter and the envelope and—if Kyle had been generous enough—*a return address.*

He ambled his way across the relatively small room, a painful welt rising in his throat, eyes burning with tears. He grabbed the letter, the envelope.

Delacroix Ave
Lagharrow, Tennessee

"Lagharrow," he whispered.

No street number. No zip code. And no sooner had he begun reading the letter than from outside the shuttered window came a sound. A groan. Not from

human or animal but of something like steel bending
right before it broke. The bedroom's enshadowed corners squirmed, the candlelight sputtered, and a smoky
phantom scent tickled his nostrils. He crossed the room,
opened the blinds, let in the sun-smothered glow. Across
the expanse of backyard danced motes in ascending
boles. And the moon

(*a roving eye*)

bled its pallid deadlight. Around its face were dark
constellations like caravans of wandering spirits. An
ectoplasmic miasma of celestial decay. Glitching astronomical bodies blanketed across that gloomy yet many-
hued pane of seemingly extraterrestrial firmament of an
uncomfortably low-hanging impression. That which
were spattered across its bleak horizon were dead stars,
pale suns, blood moons, and blots of strange black that
if one were to gaze too deeply upon, "*well . . . never you
mind that, Mom. And yet these are only placeholder
words: one speculates that the sky-stained pictures of
cosmic anomalies are a few clicks greater than the third
dimension.*"

The voice. That speaker. Garbled static from a
faraway, far, far away galaxy. Sexless and monotone,
inhuman and terrible.

"*But that's only superstitious thinking, the kind that
you and Wallace are subject in believing,*" said the
terrible voice.

And at the mention of his name Wallace spun
around.

Above Elisa's withered corpse, little more than a
skeleton now, spirals of *moony dreamlight* uncoiled
themselves from the ceiling—from whatever resided
beyond the ceiling—in serpentine fibers of a grotesque
ribbedness. At their tips were bulbous forms of
antimatter where they spake from orifices resembling

cetaceous blowholes. Said . . .

II

. . . ONE DOES NOT IMMEDIATELY SUSPECT *the old river-bottom town was haunted—well, maybe not haunted but strangely charmed. In the quaint valley tucked away in the Tennessean mountains, Lagharrow has about it a wayward romanticism of an unknown era, perhaps in which that has never before existed, not anywhere on this planet, not at any historical era: an autumnal apotheosis, an unreachable vista in man's memory of a nostalgia of some dead dreamer. When I first came here—in fact, almost accidentally; it was as if I was called here in a dream and didn't remember the dream upon waking but only remembered* the shape of the call—*a disheartening enchantment about the town had burrowed under my skin and crafted in me a seemingly incurable sense of* unease . . . *and something else besides.*

I think this unease is easily attributed to the town's geographical layout, its never-ending autumnal chill (even in the summer, it's cold), and its macabre history. Looking at the town in a bird's-eye view, you'd be able to see the mountain-caressed town in two, maybe three, distinct regions.

Exhibit one: *the charred remains on the eastern side. These splotches of historic suburbs look like an unfinished dream of some pyromaniac who had awoken against his will and was unable to finish his life's work—an aborted brick- and woodwork skeleton in a limbo of blackened rot and disintegrating foundations. A gangrenous scent of skunky woodsmoke seems to haunt this locale. (There I go using* that word *again.) When I asked*

142

a local man how the fire had started, he mentioned that in autumn of 1862—which has to do with the origins of their festival, Nocturnium—*rioters had set torch to a church and the fire went out of control and burned a large portion of the town and killed hundreds of people and most of them were from the church. The rioters had barred the doors. (Pretty twisted, I know. But when Daisy—I'll get to her later—explained it to me, it seemed mostly justified, considering the year it had happened and all its nasty political implications.) Afterward, a sort of* exodus *occurred and only a handful of residents remained. Most of these families are still here today in some way, shape, or form. In the early evenings, when I go on my walks with Daisy (a habit I've unconsciously picked up from Wallace, and a good one I might say), the soot-blackened bones of that derelict church casts burgundy shadows when the setting sun touches it just right (as Wallace might say,* It gives me the heebie-jeebies*). Looks like a ribcage of some petrified beast from olden times—not a dinosaur, per se, but something greater, something almost . . .* mystical. *It's very . . . yes, again, it's that word.*

Two*: the portions of the original town on the south- and westside—untouched by flames, but mostly a ghost town—you'll find abandoned shells of grist mills and blacksmith shops where, undoubtedly, dead shimmers dully walk their halls, stirring up dust and spiderwebs and memories. However, the northside is* mostly *barren. There is a church, not to mention the* only *church; a stiff mountainside rears it like a misshapen tidal wave made of rich, virid earth.*

And three*: not necessarily the* heart *of Lagharrow but the* liver. *A river separates this area of Lagharrow with the rest of the town. It can easily be mistaken for an island, depending on the sightline from which you view*

143

this eccentric enclave, but it stretches into the mountain in its northern regions. Across the river is where the Festival of Nocturnium takes place. Crowded houses—more like shacks—lean with an eastward tilt around the river-bending edges; two very old fraying bridges tiredly arch over the river—one of them you can barely drive across, the other you can barely walk across; and, at the heart of the liver, a tall churchless belltower coiled to its pinnacle by flowery plants. It's a sight to behold in the evenings. Daisy calls it the Finger of the Witch. The story goes something like this: immediately after the 1862 rebellion—literally the next day, if legend has any merit—the tower's construction had begun. It's said that the bones of the slave master—Simon Delacroix—and all of his supporters—the ones who died in the fire—are buried underneath. Sometimes I think the surrounding park smells like charred carrion.

I'm thinking about writing a book about Lagharrow. I know you're a reader, and you've always told me I should use my writing for something other than what you call "Twitter feuds," so here it is. Think it's good so far? I think it is. But I actually don't care what you think.

Daisy told me I should write to you, Mom. Thank her, not me. I didn't want to at first, but since the Festival is nigh they took away our phones. I guess that's something they do. The customs of Nocturnium are pretty strict and very hippy (strict hippies: a paradox, right?). Right up Wallace's alley (the strictness part, not the hippy part). It's funny how desperate and bored people get when they don't have their phones, and writing to the person they despise most sounds like the only satiating form of mindless distraction that appeals to them.

I haven't forgiven you.

You're wrong.

You're worse than a hypocrite.

Mixing your religion with politics is hurting a lot of people. You can take your fucking moral high ground and stick it somewhere. I'm writing to you for me, not you, and the Festival starts soon and it's spooky outside and I just need someone to talk to who isn't Daisy—she, being a local, just doesn't understand—and you are better than no one, I guess.

If you could only see what I'm seeing right now, Mom.

On some nights, in some portions of the overhanging cosmos above the town, are refracted obscurities from some faraway but unreachable horizon. These extracosmic flashes are brief—blink and they're gone—except, of course, for around the latter months of autumn when the Festival of Nocturnium nears. Then these ether images linger like superimposed psychedelic parasites of megalithic proportions. The ones whose psyches haven't yet turned to mush by mysterious night terrors—and other stranger forms of paralysis (usually those of an older generation, like Wallace—ha, ha)—call this weather phenomenon "Anterior Skies." It's beautiful, it's scary, like caravans of wandering spirits or an ectoplasmic miasma of celestial decay. Glitching astronomical bodies blanket across this gloomy yet many-hued pane of seemingly extraterrestrial firmament of an uncomfortably low-hanging impression. That which are spattered across its bleak horizon are dead stars, pale suns, blood moons, and blots of strange black that if one were to gaze too deeply upon, well . . . never you mind that, Mom. And yet these are only placeholder words: one speculates that the sky-stained pictures of cosmic anomalies are a few clicks greater than the third dimension. But that's only . . .

III

". . . HAVING SEIZURES ON THE FLOOR in that inferno of smoke and fire," Mindy Redman poetically says standing outside the remains of the Thossmacher residence, where Wallace and Elisa had lived for ten years. Only a year prior, Mindy tells us, had Elisa's son from an earlier marriage moved out.

"At first I thought maybe she had died and he'd gone all Shakespearean, you know? He's the sensitive type of man that maybe would, and I'm not saying that as a criticism, no, Mr. Thossmacher is one the nicest men you'll ever meet. That's one of the main reasons I didn't think twice about it. Didn't even put on my slippers. I just ran out like a bat out of—well, you know where—and oh Lord, that *fire*, that *smoke*. You'd've thought a demon had set it. Thank God their front door was unlocked and that I'd been there many times over the years and knew where they'd stationed poor Elisa. And, you know what, even though Wallace isn't a relatively large man—average-height, average-weight—I didn't know I was capable of lifting him. I'm a fifty-nine-year-old woman and I don't exercise, not as much as I should, but he felt like a sack of feathers. 'Adrenaline,' some might say, but it was a miracle." At this, Mindy Redman breaks down and walks away from our reporter.

Wallace Thossmacher, neighbors confirmed, was carried out of the house right before it collapsed. Mindy Redman sustained first-degree burns on her hands and feet but refused any medical treatment, Wallace was taken to the Oakland Hospital for third-degree burns, and Elisa's remains are yet to be found.

To stay updated, follow our social media platforms.

CHAPTER I

— STAR MOON FIRE WITCH —

I

AT FIVE-TEN P.M. WALLACE pulled into the parking lot.

Rosemont Motel was on a little crag cushioned against the mountainside: lush broomsedge, wild rhododendron, and blanched dogwood crawled up the grade and blended into a densely wooded embankment. Higher up was a crawling mist, eerily waterlike (if the water was molasses-slow and dark gray). And at the bottom, where wind-felled branches had raveled with dead and skeletal brush, a weed-shaped young man stood leaning against a rake like a wizard's staff and was thumb-swiping his phone. A thick joint trickling smoke in his mouth. Converse shoes, skinny jeans, oversized Bring Me the Horizon sweatshirt. Little progress had been made with the autumnal debris.

Wallace's attention was pulled elsewhere.

A man wearing a MAGA hat, tucked in flannel, and an athletic physique stepped out of his Ford pickup from across the parking lot. Michigan plate. He'd pulled in only fifteen seconds after Wallace had. They'd been highway comrades for several hours. Was that what made him feel instantly connected to the man? Wallace, still in the driver seat and staring in the sidemirror, waved. But MAGA hat didn't see the gesture. Or he just wasn't the friendly type. Immediately the athletic man found the white-textured expanse of crumbling sidewalk that seem like only a façade (a façade of *what*, he wasn't quite sure—call it a gut feeling) and began walking downhill.

Before stepping out of the Chevy and crossing the lot to the motel entrance, he double-checked the contents of his fanny pack—flashlight, phone, wallet, pocketknife, duct tape, two hundred dollars in cash, a roll of quarters, a photograph of Kyle, Elisa's unopened letter to Kyle, a scrap of paper from Kyle's letter that had been salvaged from the fire (it had likely flown out the house when the bedroom window shattered—

> *oon-engorged vista displayed aborted*
> *exoskeletons made of skin, mold, and*
> *madness. And things inhabited the*
> *starlight moonlight firelight witchli*),

and something he'd never needed until recently: a recently filled prescription of *oxcarbazepine*.

II

"HI, I'm here to check in."

"Yessir. What name's your reservation under?" said the middle-aged clerk, thick gray hair brimming his skull. On the counter stood a plaque that read NOC-TURNIUM SENTINEL AWARD 2021.

148

"Wallace," said Wallace. "Thossmacher."

"Interesting name. Hmmm. Let's see. Did you reserve through the website."

"Always do," said Wallace.

"Hmmm," said the clerk. Craning his neck up and over Wallace's shoulder and glancing in the general direction of the entrance and an EMPLOYEES ONLY side door, he said, "Give me a moment, sir. *CLAY. CLAY!*"

"Mr. Rosemont," said a small, puffy-eyed woman dusting the wall, but he either ignored her or didn't hear the woman speak and he screamed out "CLAY" again. This time when she said "John," with a nervous sort of tick, he *did* hear her and turned.

"He's still outside raking, sir."

"Oh. Well"—turning to Wallace—"sorry sir, my grandson's better with the computer."

"Is there a problem?"

"Looks like there's no reservation, sir."

"Well, I definitely made one."

"Yessir, I'm sure you did. Maybe it's stuck in limbo. You know how the interweb is—*CLAY.*"

"*John,*" said the woman.

The man—John—smiled a politician's smile and turned and said, "Lucy," and the woman—Lucy— flinched and glanced apologetically toward Wallace with what appeared to be a well-practiced subdued consternation and got back to dusting. Wallace perceived about John Rosemont some outer ridge of narcissism, something the man tried to purify, perhaps, based on

> (*Therefore, because of you*
> *the heavens have withheld their dew*
> *and the earth its crops*
> Haggai 1:10)

the Christendom paraphernalia about the walls, with church and charity—but perhaps it kept growing back, funguslike . . .

. . . *and* who *puts up Haggai passages, anyway?*

"Sorry sir, I'll try to get this squared away. What's a good number to reach you by?"

Wallace told him.

"Got it. And how many nights did you reserve?"

Wallace told him *three.*

As John Rosemont jotted down that information, Wallace pulled out Kyle's photograph and said, "Out of curiosity, have you seen this boy? He's my stepson."

John Rosemont made an unreadable face and turgidly said, "Who's to say? There's a dime a dozen-look about him. Especially in these parts." He made a vague finger-twirling gesture. "Anyway, in the meanwhile, if you take the sidewalk all the way you'll get to the old downtown area. Don't drive. You won't find parking. Lots of shops and restaurants. Don't mind the festive decorations. And, hey"—nodding toward a china receptacle—"coffee's on the house."

III

AT A DISTANCE HE TRAILED the red smudge of the MAGA hat downhill. Eventually the root-infested, corroding sidewalk—foreboding trees on either side—descended to the darkly historic expanse that Kyle had written about. Black husks of old buildings against the early evening sky. Decorating the trees and the liminal ruins—not quite urban or *country*—were adornments of oddly-hanging mutilated dolls, green Christmas lights, and circular wooden slabs with doghead-shaped insignias engraved into them, seemingly at spasmodic intervals. And housed in the charred joists of these weather- and time-fractured mausoleums in the town's all-but-abandoned outskirts were enormous, ugsome arachnids. Moveless handshapes were blackly inkish in their canopy-like webs against the setting sun.

Farther on he walked.

The ruins of a church. A rutted path of sad, leafy flagstones were swallowed by an overgrown, corruptive wall of virid broomsedge, saplings, and strange weeds, the front door hardly visible. Glass-fanged windows stained with grime. In rainbow-colored graffiti against one brick wall:

I KILLED PROFESSOR PORKCHOP HERE
22 MAY '07

An unkempt cemetery enclosed by sleety posts so tightly hugged against the solemn church that the headstones, ancient and weathered, leaned forward as if yearning to touch the consecrated walls; and far back in the cemetery, up against the mountainside, were willow saplings huddling around and weeping over their dead grandparents. Overstuffed dark-feathered birds perched themselves upon the church's fire-blackened and petrified beams, warped as though viewed through a prism— gawking and squawking half-heartedly at Wallace's onward walking mundanity. The church's shadow not only grew but seemed to *move* in the waning daylight—as if it were made of living, thickly concentrated black particles. And Kyle had been right about how their seeming to have been a shade of red in these shadows. More *bloodred* than burgundy, Walter would amend; and yes, it did give him the *heebie-jeebies*.

Farther on he walked.

Uncanny effigies sat in wicker chairs on eon-beaten porches. He may have mistaken these figures as manikins if not for their pale moon faces, that of careworn tiredness, slowly following his trajectory.

Weathered.

Leathered.

Forlorn.

When he said "good evening," they only stared under their battered and age-sagged eaves under a lidless sky. He noticed, also, that each porch had an identical burn-barrel, small and decorative, and from a distance it appeared as though the same symbol, facing the street, was imprinted in midnight black on their surfaces.

The wind picked up. Corroded weathervanes spun and screamed. Colonies of ants skittered up the drainpipes of rundown houses like upward flowing oil, hanging on for dear life against the stormy squall.

The eastside residential seamlessly transitioned into the old business district.

MAGA hat had disappeared around a bend or had entered a shop. Wallace in fact was surprised to find many middle-aged men and women walking the cozy downtown area. Most of them were well-dressed—not, as Kyle had mentioned, "*very hippy.*"

He could see from afar—over the distant river, past the (as Kyle has called it) *liver* of Lagharrow—a bleakly remote stone church, its peak harshly blotted by encroaching nightfall, standing tall and black against the upward-sloping mountainside; soon that sheet of lightlessness will drip down swallowing wholly the place of worship.

"*You must leave this place,*" a man yelled farther down the street. Wallace looked. The man looked Spanish or Italian, with a thick beard, thick eyebrows, slender frame, tall. He'd tucked a dark blue Denim button-up into black dress pants. In his hand he held what looked like a Bible. He stood in a public garden where a black metal fence strangled by noose-like vines prevented people from tumbling down the deep escarpment overlooking the enclave across the river. From this point the town zigged downward at a rightward bend. The tourists looked at the man. Some stopped. "Please, sir, why did you come here?" he asked a passerby.

A mumbled answer and an onward trajectory.

"Madam," he said uneasily. "This wretched abode teems with unholy apparitions, forsaken by any divine presence. The vestiges of Old World gods and . . . and malevolent entities, they loom in every corner. Do not be deceived by the façade of Nocturnium, for its true nature eludes your grasp."

A few beats of silence, and then:

"What is it, then?" someone blurted out.

Turning toward the speaker a little too eagerly the man said, "A place of wickedness. And death. It would be wise for you to depart this accursed place, for it is tainted by the forces of darkness. However, should you choose to remain and venture across the river, heed this warning: by the third night, you shall require a sum of one thousand dollars to . . . *endure the night.*"

Everyone laughed. And someone said, "And all you need is my credit card number," and kept walking and disappeared down one of the adjoining streets lost to Wallace's sightline.

Someone near Wallace coughed.

He turned and found an old man sitting next to a shopping cart teeming with assorted oddments under a barber pole. The old man sniffed in Wallace's direction, as if he had a bad scent.

"How are you, sir?" said Wallace.

The man stared across the street, a vacuous gaze. Wallace reached into his fanny pack and pulled out the photograph.

"I'm wondering if you—"

A thousand katydids said, "Depends on who you is," and spat out either tobacco or black spit.

"Name's Wallace, I'm just—"

"Whitest-ass name in the world's what that is."

Flustered. "And who are you, sir?"

"Nobody really but maybe Frank's fine enough."

"But—" Wallace swallowed and refrained himself.

"Hey now, can't say what I said to you back to me because I'm a black man, ain't that dandy?"

"I wasn't going to, sir—"

"Why not? Think I can't take it? That I'll cry if you apply your racial prejudices?"

"No, I just want to ask if you've seen the boy in this photograph. He's my—"

"—I ain't lookin' at no little boys—"

"—*Trashhead, get yo' half-blind curmudgeon head outta here. Scarin' away my customers.*"

The old man shambled away from the barbershop entrance pushing his grocery cart. It rattled like wind-agitated chimes. He passed the streetcorner preacher and the preacher spoke to the old man too low for Wallace to hear and reached into his pocket and handed something to him and the old man looked around before stuffing it into his pants pocket.

"Never you mind that Old Man Trashhead. He's a crazy ol' kook If there ever was one."

Wallace turned and saw an aproned middle-aged man in the doorway, lean and tall, with uncharacteristically green eyes contrasted against dark skin.

"That's an elaborate nickname," said Wallace, squinting against the windows reflecting the pale autumn setting sun.

"Well, he's got shorter nicknames. But they're less pleasant. What can I do you for, sir? A shave?"

"Well," said Wallace, raising a hand to feel his cheeks and neck, which pulled up his Reebok jacket sleeve and exposed a sliver of fire-scarred wrist that the barber couldn't help but gawk at, albeit only briefly (and not too obviously). "I suppose I do, if you take debit card. But I'm also here for another reason."

"Yessir, we got one o' those card readers," said the barber. "Let's get you situated in a chair and I'll help you with what I can but I won't with what I can't."

"Sounds fair enough."

"Come on in, sir," said the barber. He stepped aside gesturing for Wallace to enter. "Name's Rennie Cecil," said Rennie Cecil. "Call me Rennie, just Rennie."

"Wallace Thossmacher," said Wallace and shook hands with just-Rennie and followed him to a chair. Another barber sat in a dimly lit corner; a mass market paperback expertly splayed with one hand.

IV

THE BLADE WAS COLD BUT soothing against his neck. If Rennie noticed the scars on Wallace's upper chest and neck, he had a good enough poker face not to broadcast it.

"I can't quite say I've seen your stepson, Mr. Thossmacher, especially if—"

"Please, call me Wallace; Thossmacher makes me sound like a—I don't know—a James Bond villain, or a professor of European architecture."

Rennie laughed and turned to the other barber, repeating Wallace's joke, but the other man who was too invested in whatever book he was reading didn't laugh. Didn't even look up. Rennie said to Wallace: "You said that photograph is from a few years ago, yeah? What I mean is that the folk who live across the river, well . . . they got a particular *look*. Mighta looked one way then, another way now."

"A particular look?" said Wallace, throat straining against his awkwardly angled chin.

"Oh, I don't know. Colored hair, piercings, girls with short hair, boys who wear makeup. Hippy-types, carny-types, gender fluid-types: multigenerational misfits. You know what I mean. They all kind of blend together, not to sound prejudiced, but I'm fifty-five and I'm too old for that; it's confusing, so I apologize I can't be a little more helpful on that front. Can you turn your head a little. A little more. Perfect."

When Wallace turned he had a better view of the other barber. Older than Rennie but obviously a relative. Same eyes. Unpigmented patches swept across his forearms, which he wore with a rare sort of confidence. Only two specks of white, which could be mistaken as scars, decorated his neck and cheek.

"My stepson mentioned in a letter that the land north of here, across the river, has only two bridges. One you can walk, one you can drive."

"Can't," said the older barber without looking up from his book.

"Then how do you get there?"

"Ya can't," repeated the older barber.

"What Uncle Gresham is ungraciously implying—the condition of the bridges aside—is that it's invite only. Over on this side"—Rennie made a gesture—"anybody can participate in the trickled-down—in fact, *watered-*

down—festivities. But over there—where the festivities are traditional and pure (real Old Testament, someone might say, though I wouldn't because there's nothing Biblical about it)—it's invite only. Especially now. They'll turn you away."

"Especially now?"

"With the festival 'round the corner," said Uncle Gresham. "Nocturnium."

"The festival starts soon. Real soon," clarified Rennie. "Move your head a tad this way, Wallace, that's good, right there, perfect. Regarding Nocturnium—you're not the type that should be there, even if you're invited. 'Specially if you're invited."

Uncle Gresham cleared his throat, causing Rennie to glance over, inexplicably nictitating like a nervous little boy. When he did this, he nicked Wallace's neck. A noticeable gleam of sweat formed across his brow as he registered his error.

"Oh damn, let me get that. Hand slipped. Sorry, Wallace. It's on the house."

"No worries. If the shave's on the house, then I'll still pay for the conversation."

"You're too generous, but sure. Like I said, I can't say everything"—briefly glancing at Uncle Gresham—"but I'll say what I can."

"What did you mean when you said I'm not the type?"

"Like I said, Nocturnium is for the hippy-types—areligious, rebellious, arty."

"I saw a man wearing a Make America Great Again hat."

"Sure." Rennie cleared his throat as he placed some fabric on Wallace's cut. "He'll be disappointed if he's not invited—*approved*—and feel like he wasted a trip, until he realizes the trickled-down festivities over on this side is fine enough to satiate his curiosities; if he is invited, he'll regret it. Most definitely.

"Wait till after Nocturnium . . . and then look for your stepson. That's my advice."

Wallace sighed.

"We're almost finished. I'll clean up your neck hair, too. Getting crazy back there."

"Much obliged," said Wallace. "So . . . *how* would I get invited?"

Now Rennie sighed and said, "How much do you know about Nocturnium? I mean, what it's based on 'n' stuff?"

"The burning of a church and then it spread out and killed hundreds of people. Something like that. I can't remember if there was more. Unfortunately Kyle's letter was burned in a . . . um, *fire*. Ironically. If I hadn't made a mental note of this town's name I probably wouldn't have known to come here."

"And that probably would've been for the better," Rennie said quickly under his breath. "But, well, Wallace, that's just the aftermath. That's not how it was started and it's certainly not why they celebrate Nocturnium."

Gresham cleared his throat. Clapped his book shut. Stole the spotlight. Eyes cast toward where husks of dead spiders pancaked against the finger-smudged window, he said:

"My granddad was an old-school pastor—fire and brimstone-type. Maybe that's how they should all be, ya know? What does Joel Osteen do but make people feel *good* about their wickedness?" Shook his head. "Then his church burned."

Thumbing the general direction, Wallace said, "Is that the one near the cemetery?"

"Different one."

"They both burned down?"

"They *all* burned down. Ain't a black thing either—in case you're one o' those *too-excusatory* white folk—no sir, the white ones burned just the same. They'll burn on a cold day. They'll burn on a rainy one. They'll last a few years, maybe, but eventually, mmm hmm, they *burn.*"

For a moment Gresham stood there, his eyes jittering and faraway, as if listening to some trace notes of a ghost melody howling in the autumn wind. The sun was sinking lower. A crepuscule glow spread its fingers across the barber shop. During this moment of reflective silence, Rennie crossed the shop and flipped the *open* sign *closed* and from where he stood, before walking back, he said, "But not Pastor Ortega's."

Gresham jerked and turned creakily toward his nephew, as if being pulled from a daydream.

"No. Not Pastor Ortega's . . . and I might suspect in my marrow *why* that's so, but either my bones don't speak or I don't have the ears to hear them." There seemed to have been a fear-induced superstitiousness etched across Gresham's weathered face.

"Who's Pastor Ortega?" he ended up inquiring; but he really wanted to ask *what are you so afraid of?*

Gresham said, "He was outside earlier, deterring people—or *attempting to,* anyways—from Nocturnium's . . . *festivities.* His church is across the river. Can't miss it. Anyways, I'm getting sleepy, so I'll give ya an abridged story of the massacre of 1862; it's what my pa told me that his pa told him, and so on, passed on from ancestors with cotton-cut fingers sitting on porches (it's not like we magically stopped picking the fields after '63, by the way, especially *down here*—we just had to legally get paid for it) with their goslings plopped down listening wide-eyed to such a foreboding anecdote—that's why they called us that, ya know?"

"Call you what?"

"*Porch monkeys.*"

"—*oh!* I, um—"

Rennie laughed, and waving an impatient hand Gresham said, "My momma's called me worse names. Just wanted to see ya squirm a bit. Anyways, and I can't take credit for any of its moral wrongness or—what's the word?—*incredulousness.* Who knows how much is true, if *any* of it is. Some of it must be, though. I—a man with perfectly flawed human ears and tongue—am only a messenger, man."

"What happened?"

"It was autumn 1862. Allegedly the same time as it is now—so, mid-Octoberish. My ancestors were to be legally and systematically freed on the first of January 1863. But Simon Delacroix, a very wealthy European man, was openly claiming to fight the law and keep his slaves. So, well . . ." Gresham shrugged. "They tore him apart. They ate him. Drank his blood. Like some unholy communion."

A moment of silence.

Wallace laughed.

"That can't be true," said Wallace. "It would be in the history books."

"Would it?"

"Yes," Wallace said, not without a healthy dose of uncertainty. "It sounds fabricated."

"All stories are fabricated—the true ones especially."

Wallace let that sink in before responding.

"So you're saying that the slaves literally ate this Delacroix fella?"

"No, otherwise I'd be part cannibal—well, maybe *some* slaves partook, who's to say? But they who tore Delacroix limb by limb like a pack of wolves, they was his *white* servants. Guess they'd've been called 'slave sympathizers,' only he probably hadn't known it—that's to say, their scheme to betray him—until he was in more than one piece. *O' our white saviors.*" He chuckled, smiled, frowned, then licked his lips. "The festival means freedom for the festivalgoers, or so they say. But I think it represents something else, even if they don't admit as much."

"Which is?"

Looking directly at Wallace, his eyes emeralds in a sea of lowlight murk: "A festering, supercharged rebellion against the rigid order of all things—of their fathers, their country, of Yahweh." And in an almost too-low voice he said

(*apocalyptically*)

"They fantasize the void's homecoming; they want to dwell in it forever."

Both Wallace and Rennie stared at the old man, and Rennie finally said, "The point being is that we're not too fond of the goings-on during Nocturnium. We're only trying to help a man out. It won't hurt waiting several days."

"Several days?"

"Yessir. Tomorrow is Thursday, and they'll be setting it up, and the festival is Friday, Saturday, and Sunday until about—what do you think, Uncle Gresham?—three A.M. or so?"

"Mmhmm, reckon so," said Gresham, "the Devil's Hour. Their hour of rest."

"So, Wallace, you'll have an easier time to get accepted across the bridge if you wait till then. I know that's not what you want to hear, but—"

His phone rang. Nat King Cole's "Unforgettable" (it was his and Elisa's wedding song). Unknown number.

"Excuse me, gentlemen." He answered his phone. "Wallace speaking."

"*Mr. Thossmacher, this is John Rosemont at the Rosemont Inn. I apologize for taking so long—somehow your reservation got eaten by computer goblins—but I was able to get you one night here.*"

His heart sank. Tomorrow, he'd just have to make a significant amount of progress finding Kyle. Maybe find a motel in a neighboring town. "Oh."

"*Not to worry, Mr. Thossmacher, not to worry. I've called around and have been able to get you a room at the bed and breakfast on Delacroix Ave—*"

His blood froze.

"*—and an extra day is getting thrown into the deal— four days instead of three—paid from my own pocket— for the inconvenience, of course. Checkout's Monday morning at ten A.M.; however, Mr. Thossmacher, the only bad news—and I don't mind you keeping it here until you get back, and it shouldn't be too much of a hassle since everything is walking distance across the river—well, the bad news is: you'll have to keep your car here. The Nighted—I mean, the folk across the river are pretty* particular *about the number of cars and so forth. And, as it is, with Nocturnium starting up on Friday . . . you understand I hope.*"

Wallace was momentarily lightheaded, processing it all.

"Well, I thank you for going out of your way, Mr. Rosemont" (from his peripheral, Wallace noticed Gresham and Rennie exchange glances). "I only have one luggage, so I don't mind walking. Maybe they'll let an Uber—"

Rosemont cut him off. "*—nonsense, Mr. Thossmacher. My grandson Clay—the skinny, tall boy you might've seen doing yardwork—he's got an appointment* *with someone over there and he's agreed to drive you across. You two exchange numbers tomorrow after he drops you off and you call him when you're ready to leave. And I should tell you it's quite rare to be allowed to stay over there.*"

"Does that mean I'm '*invited*'?"

"So it seems, so it seems. You'll have Ms. Colstead to thank for that. Spoke to her directly."

"Thank you again, sir."

"*Yeah huh. Got your room ready, too. Swing by the front desk any time tonight.*"

"Thank you."

"*See you soon.*"

Rosemont ended the call and, with a dreamer's lack of lucidity, Wallace clumsily slipped his phone back into his fanny pack. He checked three times if he'd zipped it up. He had.

"Looks like I'm invited."

V

LIGHTHEADEDLY WALLACE LEFT THE BARBER shop. If Rennie or Gresham said anything behind his back, he didn't hear them; and he never saw them again.

"Delacroix Avenue," he whispered and turned and saw in the early dusk the festival-lit portions of land across the river.

Kyle was close; he felt it in his bones.

He made his way uphill, toward Rosemont Inn.

VI

Sniggering from blackened ruins.

Wallace walked off the sidewalk and found a foot-beaten path bisecting unkempt tall grass, where it led him through a brick archway and into an autumn-infected portion of half-burned village. He could almost hear their screams as the fire ate away at them. Could almost see their flickering manifestations. Had the rioters—Simon Delacroix's white servants, the slave-sympathizers, the "white saviors"—barred these doors, too? The partially intact attic gables garbled with moon-kissed mania.

And Kyle had been right about another thing: the area seemed to have been

(*haunted*)

stained by a skunky woodsmoke. He wasn't sure why but it made him ill at ease.

Silhouettes that might have been mistaken for black saplings swaying in the wind, if not for the windlessness of the night and their giggling, stood huddled together under a desolate windmill drenched in starlight. Dangling from the long rotor blades were what looked like dead babies. A small red glow passing between them—the silhouettes, not the dolls.

"Hey kids," said Wallace in his best friendly dad voice (something he considerably excelled at).

"Oh shit," one of the silhouettes muttered.

The small red glow disappeared.

"I wasn't expecting it to get so cold in Tennessee," said Wallace.

"We're in a valley, man," one of the teens said, a biracial boy with a wide Jack-O-Lantern grin. For a heart-stopping moment Wallace thought he was Kyle. He wasn't. Kyle had darker skin, a straighter nose, and no gaps in his teeth. He had Elisa's smile.

"You have a professorial aura, mister." A small mousy-looking girl had said this, giggling. He noticed her sparkly acrylic nails as she puffed a vape pen.

"I'm not a professor," said Wallace.

The teens—perhaps a bit older, in their early twenties now that his eyes had adjusted to the moonlight—laughed at that. It was as if he was the butt of a prophetically profound joke.

He pulled out the photograph.

"My stepson is around your ages. He's twenty-two. I know he was here last year. I just don't know where he's at now. Can you please take a look?"

"I know *all* the boys," said the mousy girl, and the others laughed (one said, "I don't think *know* is the right word," but the innuendo went over Wallace's head). She crossed over to Wallace, the mousy girl did, her fringe of brown hair dancing over a small forehead. A scent of cotton candy and weed and mint and something nascent. Gooseflesh ran across his left arm when she gingerly ran a clawed finger against his shoulder, and leaning over for a better look of the photograph she brushed her budding breasts against his side. "I don't know who *he* is," said the girl.

"Why'd you say it like *that*?"

The small girl walked away from him backward with a gymnast's grace, as if on tightrope, her big blue eyes never leaving his as she said, "Their *mind is a festive corpse, free of axiomatic chains of humanness clay and wine. Rebelling against* their *form,* they *will embrace maternal night. And—when* they *do, and* they *will—we will accept* them," and when she finished talking she turned and kissed a girl open-mouthed, as if that was some kind of punchline or point.

One of them whispered

(*I'm afraid of*)

"Eric Eel" as if in prayer, causing his heart to stammer.

(*They're going to eat him*)

"Eric? Who's Eric?"

He felt a different kind of gooseflesh crawl up his neck.

They laughed.

"Is something funny?"

"Why are you looking for Kyle?" said a boy with purple eyeliner and lipstick. His face was long and thin and jaundiced, reminding Wallace of one of Kyle's childhood friends. A boy named Joel.

"You do know him?"

Purple eyeliner: "*Him*?"

Biracial boy: "Fuck this guy."

Tattooed girl (or boy): "Let's just get to Joshua's."

"Yeah": collective agreement.

They started walking away and Wallace pleaded. "Wait. Elisa—his mother—she . . . she passed. And he doesn't know it yet. Please wait, just talk to me."

Biracial boy, without stopping, without turning: "There you go again. And if that's the way his momma talked to them, then I hope she had ass cancer and that it turned that bigoted bitch inside-out."

Stunned.

Cold.

Irritated.

But mostly confused.

"Egregious little punks," said Wallace, not knowing if "egregious" meant what he thought it did. "She was a good woman, you don't know what you're talking about, *I* don't know what you're talking about, and I need to know where my stepson is right this minute.

"Hey! I'm talking to you kids."

They kept walking.

"Hey!"

He reached for the biracial boy's sweatshirt, pulled him around, and something swept across his face. A fist. Wallace stumbled back, twisted, fell facedown, "look'it that goddamned fanny pack," "hehehaha," "open it—"

"—stop." *Ahp.*

But they didn't *ahp* and the sky blistered with heat lightning . . . hand-shaped flashes . . . in betwixt, in the primordial black of night, flapped wings dark and—

Hungry.

"*Hehehaha hahahe hahahahe.*"

Snarling.

Cachinnating hyenas all.

The tattooed boy (or girl) pressed his or her knee into the small of his back and Wallace grimaced.

"Please, stop, my medicine."

"Oxcarbawhatinthehellisthis?"

"Probably Viagra."

"Come on, take his money, let's go."

"Stop! *SOMEONE HELP!*"

"Shut his fucking face."

Something hard fell onto his head.

Warm fluid filled his mouth. Specks of light sizzled across the bleak horizon where dead stars, pale suns, blood moons, and

(*he's twitching*
shit, we killed him
someone's coming, hurry)

blots of strange black spread outward in eons in every direction. Then the snide teens scattered: pool balls each finding a hole in the form of alleyways, doors, and—in the cases of a small twentysomething with long, literally dirty blond hair, and a denim-clad black girl (maybe a boy)—*literal holes* in the decaying ruins. And there lay Wallace, a lonesome and jittering white ball.

Governing things inhabited the starlight moonlight firelight witchlight, and a chorus:

"For when the mutilated melody of whip-poor-wills is heard in the reachless void of brooding mountainside—when the river-bottom country swells joyfully with nostalgic music of Halloween wind—when the liminal beauty of dead leaves, woeful clouds, and chilled air is free of dogmatic paternal hands—when pale suns and blood moons breathe life into our marrow and into our souls—we will offer our sacrifices to the festering flesh and open our formlessness to the maternal night . . .

". . . these are the words . . ."

Instagram: @CFPage_Author
X (formerly known as **Twitter**): @CFPage_Author
Facebook: www.facebook.com/CFPageBooks

And—pretty please with sugar on top—use **#OrphansOfTheAtercosm** on **X** and **Instagram**, should you post a review or are trying to boost the signal (even if it's a 1-star); I'm going to be campaigning hard for a Bram Stoker Award nomination for **Superior Achievement in a Collection**, and I'll need your help.

If you enjoyed *Orphans of the Atercosm*, then please consider my debut novel, *Native Fear*, which is a contender for **Facebook's Books of Horror's 2024 Indie Author Brawl** (if you're a fan of horror and aren't part of that group, you need to be). Being in the top 32, which will be announced in March—in which group members get to vote on their favorite books—could at least get enough eyes on *Native Fear* so it could slip into the mainstream, help me find a literary agent, and get *Native Fear* optioned for film.

My literary mission statement is to bridge the gap between weird and mainstream; to smash open the echo-chambers and overthrow the horror gatekeepers; and to *politely slap* the Big 5 publishers and their imprints in the face, and let them know that horror can be a financially viable genre if they let horror gamers into the club by marketing books *to* them. By publishing books *for* them. *Resident Evil*, *Bioshock*, *Silent Hill*, *Dead Space*, *Bloodborne, The Last of Us*—gamers will read books that scratch their itches. Gamers aren't illiterate.

Made in the USA
Columbia, SC
19 November 2024

47094043R00107